THE FAMILY I ONCE KNEW

By

FENIX SANDERS

TABLE OF CONTENTS

THE CURE

The fluorescent lights hummed like a warning—low, constant, sterile. I walked between two Secret Service agents, their eyes never stopping, even down here. Especially down here. The corridor stretched ahead, white walls too clean, too quiet, like the world hadn't already started rotting outside.

I kept my hands at my sides to stop them from shaking.

To my left, glass separated us from clusters of scientists—some typing furiously, some standing still. One man pressed his forehead against the glass, eyes wide, like he wanted to say something but forgot how. A woman was crying while she entered data into a terminal, her tears sliding off her chin onto the keyboard. She didn't wipe them away.

I didn't know her name. But I'll remember her face longer than most.

"This is where it starts," I told myself, though deep down I knew that wasn't true. It had already started. We were just the last ones pretending we still had a chance to stop it.

The end of the hallway was a wall of steel. The final door. Thick enough to take a missile. Red lights blinked along its edges, waiting for codes only a few people still alive could give. One of the agents stepped forward and began the authentication. The other turned slightly toward me.

"President Hector, once we're inside, the scientists will brief you. They'll give you the vial. Echo Black should be arriving shortly after."

I nodded, jaw tight. I hadn't spoken much in the last hour. Not since I'd seen what was left of New York through the convoy window.

A hiss of pressure escaped as the massive door began to unlock. Each clang of machinery felt heavier than the last.

As it creaked open, I realized something I couldn't shake.

This might be the last quiet place left on Earth.

The lab was too quiet.

Not silent—machines whirred, monitors blinked—but quiet in a way that felt... afraid. Like, even the walls knew how close we were to losing.

Dr. Kellerman met me halfway through the sterile chamber. Thin, pale, sweat already breaking at his temples. His lab coat looked like he'd been wearing it for days. Maybe he had.

"Mr. President," he said, voice cracked and hoarse. "It's ready."

He led me to a containment pedestal. There it sat—inside a clear titanium case, suspended in a magnetic field. A vial no longer than my finger. Its liquid pulsed faintly, not glowing exactly, but alive. Like it was breathing.

"This is the only one?" I asked, even though I already knew the answer.

Kellerman nodded. "It's stable, finally. But the replication process—what's left of our facilities—won't survive another breach. You have to get it to the west bunker. They still have the tools. They still have the people."

I stared at it. One vial. The weight of seven billion people condensed into half an ounce of silver-blue fluid.

Another tech walked up, holding what looked like a handcuff. It was matte black, biometric-coded. Kellerman took it and turned to me.

"It has to be with you at all times. We engineered it to lock to your wrist—no one else can remove it, not even you. If your pulse stops, the cuff injects a neutralizing compound so the virus doesn't get it. We're not taking any chances."

My throat was dry. "And if I get torn apart before that happens?"

He didn't answer.

The cuff clicked into place. Cold against my skin. Final.

The case hissed open. The vial was loaded into the cuff by steady hands. I didn't look away, even when the lock snapped shut and the green light blinked to life on the side.

It was mine now.

My burden. My curse. My duty.

"Echo Black?" I asked, finally breaking the silence.

"They're inbound. Family unit. Highly trained. You'll be in good hands."

I clenched my fist once, testing the weight of the vial on my wrist. It felt heavier than it looked.

Outside the blast doors, I heard the first sound of boots.

Echo Black had arrived.

The sound of boots echoed before I saw them—four distinct rhythms, each one a piece of a larger machine.

The door hissed open, and in stepped a man who looked like he could snap a steel pipe in half just by looking at it. Easily six feet tall, broad as a tank, built like a sledgehammer with a heartbeat. His eyes were sharp but relaxed, like he'd seen every possible kind of hell and decided none of it was worth flinching over.

He smirked the moment our eyes met.

"Viper Two," he said. "But Charles works fine. As long as you don't make me call you 'Your Excellency' or some royal crap."

I opened my mouth, but before I could speak, a woman stepped in beside him—smaller, lean, but commanding in her own right. Her brown hair was pulled back tight, the gray roots like a crown of experience. Her gaze was pure calculation.

"Bacon One," she said calmly. "Sheila. Navigator and intelligence. Also, I apologize in advance for everything my husband says from here on out."

"Lies," Charles said, not missing a beat. "I'm a national treasure."

"She means like Chernobyl," a new voice cut in, strolling through the doorway with an easy swagger.

The third member entered without so much as a glance around. Same height as Charles, but leaner, more wiry. There was a mischievous glint in his eye—like he couldn't wait to find something to take apart, or blow up, or both.

"CJ Sanders," he said. "Diablo Four. Fixer, hacker, engineer. Basically, I keep the rest of these old people alive."

Sheila rolled her eyes. "You're thirty-two."

"Exactly. And that's ancient for a gamer."

"Not a good gamer," the final voice said. Quiet. Controlled.

Shaun stepped into the room like a shadow with muscle. Taller than CJ by a hair, but built with a heavier frame. No smirk. No sarcasm. Just stillness, with eyes like cold steel and a jaw clenched a little too tight. He didn't look at me—he scanned the lab like he expected it to explode at any second.

"Sparky Three," he said. "Shaun. Forward assault."

CJ leaned over to whisper, loud enough for me to hear anyway. "He's the moody one. Thinks he's Superman."

"I heard that," Shaun replied without looking at him.

"Good. It was for you."

Charles cleared his throat. "Boys."

They both fell quiet instantly.

I couldn't help it—I smiled, just slightly. For the first time in weeks, I wasn't surrounded by stiff suits or pale-faced scientists. These were real people. A family. There was something grounding about that. Familiar, even at the end of the world.

Dr. Kellerman stepped forward, clearly unsure how to engage with this kind of energy. "This is… Echo Black. Your escort team."

"I figured," I said. "The code names gave it away."

Sheila cracked a tiny grin.

Kellerman motioned toward me. "The President now carries the only known stable cure. It is locked to his wrist and cannot be removed. Your job is to get him to the western extraction zone. Your helicopter is twelve minutes out."

Charles's tone shifted—snapping into command mode instantly. "Copy that. Routes?"

Sheila stepped forward, already pulling up maps on a compact wrist tablet. "There's a corridor system that'll get us topside. Once we're airborne, we follow the path north across cleared zones. Then drop into the black line and extract at Grid Delta. If we're lucky, we won't hit a swarm until the outskirts."

CJ looked at me. "Define 'lucky.'"

Shaun added without looking up, "Lucky means we die fast."

I stared at the four of them—this odd blend of discipline and dysfunction. Armor, weapons, tight formations… and banter that never stopped.

They weren't perfect.

They were better.

Charles turned to me, his face serious again. "You stick close to us, Mr. President. You run when we run. You stop when we stop. And if CJ starts talking too much, feel free to shoot him."

"Hey!" CJ said. "This is why I don't build you guys exosuits."

Charles snorted. "Like we'd trust you with a soldering iron."

Sheila stepped in smoothly. "We'll protect him, Charles. That's the mission."

Charles looked back at her, softer for just a moment.

"I know," he said.

I looked down at the vial strapped to my wrist. Glowing faintly. Steady.

Twelve minutes until takeoff.

Twelve minutes until we leave the last quiet place on Earth.

They moved like a well-oiled machine—cracking jokes, trading jabs, checking gear. But underneath it all, there was something unmistakable. A tension they weren't showing me. A rhythm you only develop when you've fought and bled together, again and again.

CJ dropped to a knee beside a supply crate, pulling out a diagnostic tablet and checking something on his rifle's smart-link.

"Shaun, your comm's still glitched. Try not to die before I fix it mid-firefight, yeah?"

Shaun didn't look up as he slid a fresh mag into his rifle. "I won't need it. You'll be behind me."

"Damn right," CJ grinned, then turned to Sheila. "Mom, he's being mean again."

Sheila smirked as she adjusted her wristpad. "I told you boys to play nice in front of the President."

"Pretty sure the world ending gives me a pass," CJ replied.

Charles stood a few feet away, silently inspecting a long matte-black M4 rifle, his fingers moving with practiced precision. One glance at his wife and sons was all it took for him to sigh.

"Let 'em talk. Helps them focus."

He looked at me suddenly—eyes piercing. "You ever fired a weapon, sir?"

I hesitated. "I did a few training ops in college. And a photo op at a range in 2023, but I doubt that counts."

"Doesn't," Shaun said flatly, slapping a mag into his sidearm.

CJ offered me a pistol from the crate. "Take it anyway. It's for you, not the press."

I reached out and took it—heavier than I expected. Cold.

"Safety's here. Squeeze, don't pull," CJ added. "And if I die, you inherit my drone."

"I didn't know you had a drone."

"Exactly. It's very sneaky."

I caught myself smiling again. That made three times in one hour. Unthinkable lately.

Behind them, the low whine of rotor blades started to echo through the facility. It wasn't loud yet, but it was building.

Charles glanced at his watch. "Five minutes."

Dr. Kellerman stepped forward, face pale. "The pilot's name is Rowe. Former Air Force. You'll exit through the north corridor and load from the platform roof. It's the last confirmed safe route."

"Confirmed by who?" CJ asked.

"People who didn't come back," Kellerman replied.

CJ gave a mock salute. "Comforting."

The team gathered by the steel exit doors, forming up like they'd done this a thousand times. I stood a step behind, awkward in my civilian coat, the pistol tucked tight against my ribs. I didn't belong in this picture—but I was part of it anyway.

"Stay between me and Sheila," Charles instructed. "We move fast, we don't stop, we keep you breathing. That's the plan."

"And if things go sideways?" I asked.

"Then we kill everything that isn't smiling at you," CJ said.

"Correction," Shaun added, "we kill everything. No exceptions."

The door hydraulics hissed, and a blast of cold air hit my face.

Above us, the helicopter was getting louder now—closer. The dull thump-thump-thump of rotor blades slicing the air. My heartbeat matched the rhythm.

Sheila gave Charles a long look. Just a flicker of it. One of those silent glances married people use when they've said everything they needed to years ago.

He nodded.

CJ caught it too. "You two gonna get all mushy right before we go airborne?"

Sheila didn't miss a beat. "Only if we survive the ride."

Charles smirked. "Then I'm definitely not dying today."

They stepped out together—black armor gleaming under harsh overhead lights. The hallway led into a wide stairwell, and from there… the platform. I could already see daylight creeping through the cracks in the blast doors ahead.

Shaun took point, rifle up, laser cutting across corners. Silent. Fluid. Not cocky—ready.

I walked behind him, surrounded by ghosts in body armor. A family I barely knew.

The sound of the helicopter was thunderous now—our ride home. Our escape.

And somehow, I already knew it wouldn't go as planned.

2

FIRE FROM THE SKY

The city stretched out below us like a shattered memory.

From this height, it looked almost peaceful—rows of silent streets, unmoving cars, sun-bleached buildings. But it wasn't peace. It was aftermath.

And then we saw them.

"East side's crawling," Sheila said from her seat, tapping the tablet in her lap. A live satellite feed flickered—glitched, corrupted—but enough came through. "That's a horde. Two hundred, maybe three."

I leaned over despite myself and looked out the window. What I saw didn't feel real.

They were everywhere. Hundreds of them—running, staggering, clawing over one another. Some missing limbs, others grotesquely bloated, mutated beyond anything I'd seen in the reports. A few sprinted like animals, crashing into buildings and smashing through glass as they chased something…

Someone.

"There—!" CJ pointed through the opposite window. "That alley. Holy hell. That guy's alive!"

Sure enough, one man sprinted across a narrow intersection, dragging a woman behind him. Blood covered his shirt, and the woman's leg was twisted wrong, but they ran like their lives depended on it—because they did.

A child followed them. Limping. Falling behind.

Shaun muttered, "They're not gonna make it."

I wanted to look away. I didn't.

They turned a corner—too slow.

The dead caught them before they reached the end of the block. It wasn't a fight. It was a flood. Bodies consumed them. Screams rose even above the thump of rotors.

CJ stared for a second longer than the others. Then he looked away and shook his head.

"Damn," he muttered. "I hate being right."

Shaun just reloaded his rifle with a metallic click.

"That wasn't a skirmish," Charles said, arms crossed, eyes fixed on the scene below. "That was a trap. They were herding them. Seen it before."

"Biters are dumb," CJ replied. "But mutations? They learn."

"Not like this," Sheila said. "They're adapting faster than we calculated. The ones leading the herd had fused arms, enlarged torsos—one was carrying a pipe like a club. They're not just mutating—they're evolving."

A thick silence followed.

I gripped the frame beside me. "You're saying this is going to get worse."

Charles glanced at me. "Mr. President… this isn't the worst. Yet."

Then, just as fast as the silence had crept in—

CJ cracked a grin. "So on a scale of one to 'completely boned,' where are we?"

"CJ," Sheila warned.

"What?" he asked innocently. "Just trying to gauge how much ammo I should cry over wasting."

Shaun rolled his eyes. "You'd cry over a donut if it had the wrong glaze."

"Wrong glaze is serious, Sparky. You wouldn't understand."

Charles didn't even look away from the window. "You two done measuring your brains?"

CJ raised an eyebrow. "Define 'done.'"

Another low chuckle passed through the cabin. For a minute, it was almost like the world wasn't ending.

Then the pilot's voice broke through the headset:

"Eyes open. We're approaching the drop zone perimeter. Turbulence ahead. Something's messing with the air currents."

Sheila frowned. "Could be the fire. I'm reading elevated thermal pockets—some of them aren't natural. Rooftop blazes maybe, or…"

"Or?" Shaun pressed.

"Or mutated activity that's generating its own heat."

Charles turned to us. "Everyone lock in. Weapons tight. No masks off until we confirm air is clean. President stays between me and Bacon One."

"Yes, sir," CJ and Shaun said in perfect sarcastic sync.

"Mock me again and I'll make you share a sleeping bag," Charles added.

CJ made a face. "With Shaun? Gross."

Shaun didn't miss a beat. "I sleep cold. Hope you like cuddling."

As the banter faded, I looked back out the window, past the chaos.

We were flying over hell… and the worst part wasn't what we saw—it was knowing we were heading straight into it.

And for the first time since this mission started…

I was afraid they wouldn't make it.

Suddenly something felt wrong.

The sky was wrong.

It turned orange too quickly. Not a sunset, not firelight—something else. Something brighter, hotter, rising from the streets below like a goddamn signal flare from hell.

Sheila's voice cracked through the headset: "Thermals just spiked—ten blocks ahead. We've got something big."

"Define big," Charles snapped.

"I don't know," she replied, already tapping furiously at her tablet. "It's not a fire. It's moving. Something's—"

The helicopter lurched.

Not turbulence. Not wind. Something hit us.

CJ shouted, "What the hell was that?!"

Then we all saw it.

Below us, rising like a monster out of myth, a thing—a walking abomination—stood on top of a collapsed office tower, framed in smoke and flame. Ten feet tall, easily. Its flesh was split with glowing orange veins like molten cracks in rock. One arm was normal. The other? Fused with rusted steel and rebar. A makeshift club of bone and debris.

And in its other hand—it held a chunk of concrete the size of a car door.

"Oh, that's new," CJ said, stunned.

Shaun leaned over. "It's aiming."

Before I could even process the word, the thing hurled the slab.

"Evasive! Evasive!" the pilot screamed, yanking the stick sideways.

Too late.

The chunk of debris smashed into the tail rotor with a deafening crunch. The whole world flipped sideways.

We were spinning. Metal screamed. Red lights flared in the cabin. Someone yelled "Brace!"—maybe Charles, maybe Shaun. Didn't matter. The floor became the ceiling, and gravity forgot how to work.

Sparks exploded around us. I felt my body lift, slam, bounce. CJ slammed into the opposite wall. Sheila clutched her harness with white-knuckled grip. Shaun was dragging me toward the bulkhead, teeth gritted. Charles was barking orders I couldn't hear over the noise.

Then—

Impact.

The crash was a roar, a crush, a blur of steel and fire. The helicopter slammed down hard on its side, scraping across pavement. Windows shattered. Something heavy—maybe the rear hatch—ripped away. Then blackness swallowed everything.

Silence.

Smoke.

Flames crackling.

A groan of bending metal.

I opened my eyes.

We were down.

The cabin was on its side. Sheila was groaning, blood running down her forehead. CJ was pinned under a dislodged seat. Shaun was already pushing wreckage off his chest, coughing.

I tried to move—pain screamed through my shoulder. My vision doubled.

The pilot was still in his seat, upside down, coughing, blood on his lips.

"Mr. President!" he barked, his voice sharp. "Sir! You with me?!"

"I'm—here—" I croaked.

He unbuckled, dropped down, stumbled over debris, and grabbed my arm. "We gotta move. You can stand?"

"I—I think—"

"Good enough. Come on—"

A shadow passed the broken side door.

Then another.

And another.

CJ gasped, "They're already here."

Outside the wreckage, they came.

Biters. At least twenty. Maybe more. Crawling, sprinting, limping—drawn by the crash like wolves to blood.

The pilot turned, putting himself between me and the breach. "Go! GO!"

He shoved me hard toward the bent emergency door, where Shaun and Charles were clearing a path.

Then they swarmed him.

I turned just in time to see the pilot fire his sidearm twice— before disappearing under a pile of shrieking, tearing bodies.

"No!" I shouted—but Charles was already pulling me through the wreckage.

"We can't save him," he growled. "Move, Hector. Now."

The pilot's scream was cut off mid-breath.

And just like that, we were in the fire, the smoke, the teeth.

The world had caught fire.

I stumbled through the shattered remains of the helicopter, my ears ringing with a high-pitched whine that drowned out the screams. Smoke clung to my lungs like tar. The air was thick with the stench of burning metal, blood, and rot.

Then the noise hit me—all at once.

Gunfire everywhere.

Short, sharp bursts. Controlled. Military.

Mixed with the wet, animal shrieks of the undead.

"SIX O'CLOCK—DOWN!"

Shaun's voice cut through the chaos.

I hit the ground as his rifle barked above me. The three closest biters collapsed mid-sprint, heads exploding in a fine red mist. Shaun stepped over me like a shield, already turning to scan for the next threat. His expression was cold, focused. Not a trace of fear.

Charles appeared from the smoke, dragging CJ by the back of his plate carrier. "Diablo Four's hit but breathing!"

"I'm fine," CJ snapped, holding a bloodied arm. "Bullet nicked me or something. Not a biter. Stop manhandling me."

"Move your ass or I'll really manhandle you," Charles growled.

"Boys, shut up!"
Sheila's voice came from the right, low and fast. "West flank's collapsing. They're circling!"

From her position behind a broken slab of concrete, she fired in quick bursts, picking off a pair of infected as they tried to flank us. Her hands moved like a machine, no hesitation, even with blood dripping down the side of her face.

"Mr. President, stick to me," Charles barked. "I'll get you out of here alive even if I have to carry you on my damn back."

"I can move!" I shouted.

"Good. Because if you slow down, I will slap you. Let's go!"

They weren't just fighting.

They were dancing.

A brutal, violent, choreographed dance. CJ patched up his own arm mid-movement, flipped his rifle, and covered Shaun without even looking. Sheila gave precise updates on incoming waves, calling coordinates between shots. Charles kept a hand on me at all times—guiding, pushing, shielding. Bullets passed within inches. One biter got so close I could smell its rotted breath before Charles put a knife through its skull with terrifying speed.

The dead didn't stop.

They came in twos, then fives, then ten at a time. Every shot Echo Black fired had to count. There was no backup. No second helicopter. Just us… and hell.

Shaun ducked beside CJ, slammed a fresh mag into his rifle, and muttered, "Bet you miss fixing radios right about now."

CJ grimaced. "Bet you miss not smelling like someone lit a morgue on fire."

"We're not done!" Sheila shouted. "More coming through the storefront!"

We turned. Another wave—fifteen, maybe more—rushed from a shattered department store, half of them limping, the others sprinting. One was missing its jaw. Another had three arms. All of them screamed like banshees.

"They're cutting us off!" I yelled.

"Not if I can help it!" CJ reached into his pack, pulled out something cobbled together with tape, wires, and righteous anger. "Homemade flashbang. Not safe. Not legal. Definitely effective."

"CJ, no!" Sheila started.

CJ grinned and lobbed the device through a shattered window. "TOO LATE!"

BOOM.

A thunderclap of light and sound ripped through the street. Half the biters dropped to the pavement, stunned or screaming. The rest staggered in confusion. It gave us the gap we needed.

"MOVE!" Charles yelled. "Down the alley—tight quarters. Easier to defend!"

We ran.

I didn't look back.

I couldn't.

Because if I did…

I'd see the pilot's body torn apart in the wreckage.

I'd see what waited in the firelight.

We tore through the alley like it owed us blood.

The walls were too close. Cracked brick on one side, chain-link fence on the other. Trash bins. Scattered debris. The perfect funnel for the dead.

"Weapons tight—watch your corners!" Charles shouted.

"Clear left!" Shaun barked.

"Right side—dumpster movement!" Sheila responded, already sweeping her rifle that way.

"Shadows at the end of the alley," CJ called. "Three incoming—wait, no, five."

They moved like a unit possessed. Each voice is quick and exact. They didn't yell over each other—they flowed. One move fed the next. Every step felt rehearsed, like they'd done this a thousand times before.

And I—

I was just trying to keep up.

Charles was in front, leading with his M4, shoving trash and obstacles aside with raw strength. Shaun held the rear, his rifle barking in sharp bursts. CJ stuck close to Sheila—covering her as she used her tablet to map escape routes even while firing between data pings.

Me?

I had a sidearm. A SIG Sauer. Heavy in my hand.

No training. Just raw adrenaline.

But I was watching. Listening.

And then everything went sideways.

A shriek. A flash of motion.

From a doorway at our flank, a biter lunged—fast, too fast. It wasn't mindless like the others. This one still had something in its eyes. Hunger. Rage. Intelligence.

It moved like it remembered being human.

And it was going straight for Sheila.

She didn't see it. Not in time.

"BACON—LEFT!" CJ screamed, already turning, but his rifle was still mid-reload.

Time slowed.

Sheila was exposed. One step from death.

I raised my pistol.

Crack.

The gun went off in my hands before I even knew I'd pulled the trigger. The shot was ugly, clumsy—but it hit. The round took the biter clean through the temple. It collapsed in a heap at Sheila's feet, twitching.

Everything froze for half a heartbeat.

Sheila turned to me. Her eyes were wide. Shocked. Blood splatter across her cheek. She gave me a tight nod.

"Good eyes," she said simply—then turned back to firing.

No wasted words. No time for more.

"Nice shot, Mr. President!" CJ yelled as he slammed a new mag into his rifle. "We'll make a killer outta you yet!"

"Not the career I applied for!" I shouted back.

Charles looked over his shoulder, eyes scanning me. "You shoot like shit, but you saved my wife. That's two points for Hector."

I felt something settle in my chest. Not pride—fear, still—but also resolve. I wasn't just cargo anymore. Not dead weight. Maybe not a soldier… but not helpless either.

"Keep it up, Prez," Shaun said without turning. "First one's always the hardest."

Then the alley howled.

A new wave. Thirty feet ahead—climbing the fences, bursting from broken side doors. Some are still smoldering from the crash. All coming straight for us.

"Wall breach!" Charles shouted. "They're pushing both sides!"

"Funneled too tight," CJ muttered. "We can't hold a line here."

"We fall back," Sheila ordered. "Up the fire escape—now!"

Charles boosted me first. Hands like steel shoved me upward. I climbed, slipped, and grabbed the metal bars. CJ followed. Sheila was next.

Shaun didn't move.

He was still on the ground—his rifle firing short, measured bursts as the wave closed in.

"Shaun! GO!" Charles roared.

"I got it!" he barked. "Just two more—"

A screamer hit him from the side. Shaun dropped, grappled, teeth inches from his face.

Charles jumped off the ladder.

"NO!" I shouted, but it was already too late.

They were fighting again—father and son, back-to-back—crushing the last of the wave with brutal efficiency. Charles cracked one skull with the butt of his rifle. Shaun stabbed another through the eye. They moved as one. Pure violence. Pure focus.

Then they were climbing again. Covered in blood, breathing hard, but alive.

As they reached the rooftop, I realized something.

They didn't do this for glory.

They didn't even do it just for me.

They did it… because they were a family.

And families don't leave each other behind.

3

CONCRETE GRAVES

We barely made it to the rooftop.

The alley behind us was a graveyard of torn flesh and scorched bones. The sky burned a low orange, casting jagged shadows through the smoke. I leaned against the rusted air unit, trying to force breath into lungs that felt too small for my body.

"Status?" Charles barked.

"Minor wound," CJ said, wrapping a new bandage around his arm. "Still functional."

"Clear up top," Sheila said. "Vantage point's solid, but we can't stay long."

Shaun stood near the ledge, scanning the streets below with sharp eyes. "We lost them in the alley. For now."

I didn't know what to say. What could I say? I'd shot a man—thing two feet from someone's wife. I'd climbed a fire escape covered in blood. I'd watched more people die in twenty minutes than most would in a lifetime.

Then it crackled.

The radio.

At first, it was just static. Then…

"…This is Safe Zone Charlie… northeast sector… under attack… repeat, we're under attack—biters breached south wall…"

We all froze.

"…Seven of us—ammo running low—if anyone can hear this, please—we're four blocks west of Truman and 6th… God help us…"

The signal cut out. Just static.

A heartbeat passed.

Then another.

Charles looked at Sheila. "Navigation. Truman and 6th. How far?"

"Three blocks straight, one over," she said, already pulling the map up. "We can make it. But that area was marked hot during the initial sweeps."

CJ wiped grime off his forehead. "We're low on rounds. My mag's half full, Shaun's probably close to dry."

Shaun checked his gear. "Four mags left. I can stretch it."

"Could be a trap," CJ muttered. "A beacon to draw the desperate."

"Or it's seven people who don't deserve to be eaten alive," Sheila snapped.

"Enough," Charles said. "Let's make it simple."

He turned to me. "Mr. President, that's three blocks of infected territory. We move fast, loud, and burn calories we can't replace. We'll go if you order it—but it puts the cure at risk."

He didn't say it like a challenge. He said it like a man willing to die if I said yes.

I swallowed. "Let's go."

CJ gave a low sigh. "Guess I'm using that last Molotov after all."

Fifteen minutes later, we were at Truman and 6th.

Too late.

The safe zone had been a small grocery store—makeshift barricades of metal shelving and carts. Blood was everywhere. Bits of clothing. A child's shoe.

Too quiet.

We entered with weapons raised. No movement—just the buzzing of flies and the wet slap of dripping blood.

Then—a scream.

We ran toward it.

Back room. Three survivors cornered—two adults, one teen— firing pistols at the windows as hands clawed through every crack.

CJ vaulted the counter. Shaun took the right flank. Sheila opened fire through the shelves, deadly and efficient. I stayed behind Charles, who kicked the back door open with enough force to snap it off the hinges.

The infected came fast. A dozen. Two dozen.

They were already *inside*.

Shaun grabbed the teenager. "Come on, MOVE!"

Too late.

One of them—bitten—screamed as her neck was torn out. The man with her lost his mind, ran into the horde. The last one, the teen, tried to fight but—

Blood. Screams. Gunfire.

We killed every last one of them. But none of the survivors made it out alive.

Not one.

Silence returned, thick and heavy.

Shaun looked at the broken body at his feet. "They were just trying to last the day…"

Charles holstered his rifle. "We gave them a few more minutes. Bought us a breath. Bought them peace."

I leaned against the wall, heart pounding. "That was the right call."

Sheila knelt near a dropped pack. "Ammo," she said, pulling out four pistol mags. "And these—"

She held up two shortwave radios and a folded paper map with hand-drawn markings. Checkpoints. Routes. Notes.

"This was more than a safe zone," she whispered. "They were mapping the area."

CJ took it gently. "They may be gone… but they gave us something."

We were still breathing.

But the weight of failure sat heavy on our shoulders.

And somewhere beyond the fire, more were screaming.

The stench of death clung to everything.

The blood wasn't even dry.

We sat in the back room of what used to be a corner store, surrounded by broken shelves, spent casings, and the silence left behind after people stopped screaming.

Shaun was by the door, wiping his knife with a torn piece of someone's shirt. He didn't say a word. His jaw clenched so tight I thought it might snap.

CJ sat cross-legged on the dirty floor, counting rounds and muttering numbers under his breath.

Charles stood like a statue, his back to us all, staring at the street outside through a cracked window. He hadn't moved in minutes.

Sheila was next to me. She'd laid the map out on a table scarred with bullet holes, tracing the survivor's handwritten notes with a trembling finger. Her voice was steady, but I could tell—her hands weren't.

"Looks like they scouted five blocks south. Marked a hardware store with an 'S'… maybe a stash? There's also an 'X' over a bridge two streets east. Could be a no-go zone."

"Bridge probably collapsed," CJ said, setting his rifle down and stretching. "Or infested."

Charles finally spoke. "What's the nearest safe structure?"

Sheila tapped the map. "Old police precinct. Two blocks west. If the infected haven't swarmed it yet, it might have supplies… radios, weapons, armor."

CJ nodded. "Could use a re-up. I've got one full mag left for my rifle, two for my sidearm. That's it."

"Three mags left for me," Shaun said, wiping his blade one last time. "One for my pistol. Knife's sharp."

"Two mags for me," Charles said. "We'll have to get creative soon."

"I'm useless if it comes to that," I admitted, my voice low. "One half-full pistol mag. And I'm shaking."

"You're not useless," Sheila said without looking up. "You saved my life back there."

"She's right," Charles added. "And if we didn't get that map, we'd still be flying blind."

CJ tossed me a water bottle. "Hydrate. Your hands stop shaking after a while. Or you just stop noticing."

I caught it—barely—and twisted the cap. It was warm, slightly metallic, but it tasted like the best thing I'd had in days.

We passed the bottle around in silence. No one drank too much. A few gulps. A nod. Move on.

"You think we'll find anyone else alive?" I asked.

Shaun stared at me for a moment. "I think we'd better hope we don't."

"Why?"

"Because every time we find someone, they die."

His words dropped like lead.

Nobody argued.

Sheila folded the map. "We move in ten. I'll guide us to the precinct. Might be dry, might be crawling. Either way, we don't sit still."

"Agreed," Charles said. "CJ—check that survivor's radio. If it works, we'll scan on approach."

CJ held it to his ear. "Still got juice. Might even reach a few blocks out."

Then something strange happened.

Charles looked at his family. One by one. Then at me.

He exhaled.

"Good job today."

They all stared at him like he'd just announced the world was ending *again*.

"Did… did Dad just give a compliment?" CJ said.

"Check for fever," Shaun deadpanned. "Might be infected."

"I'm serious," Charles said, cracking half a grin. "Wasn't pretty, but we're alive. We moved. We adapted."

"First time for everything," Sheila murmured with a smirk.

"Still not saying thank you," CJ said, standing up.

"I wasn't fishing," Charles muttered, brushing past him. "Get your gear ready. Move out in five."

As they prepped, I found myself watching them again—not just for how they moved, but for how they leaned on each other. Sarcasm, quips, shared silence—it was all communication. All part of the same rhythm.

They weren't just trained.

They were *bonded*.

And somehow, despite the burning streets and the broken sky above us…

…I felt safer with them than I ever had behind a podium.

We were down to scraps.

Charles unzipped the last of our packs, laid out what ammo remained on the floor. It wasn't much. Just a few loaded mags, some loose rounds, and a small pouch of pistol ammunition that CJ claimed "wasn't even worth the brass it's made from."

Still, Charles divided it like it mattered.

"Two mags each for rifles," he said. "One for sidearms. No more spray and pray. Controlled bursts, center mass."

Shaun took his share wordlessly. CJ grunted. Sheila clipped hers in and checked the chamber.

Then Charles slid two full mags across the table toward me.

"I don't need this much," I said.

"You do if we die," he replied. "And you're not dying."

Before I could argue, Shaun stepped forward, holding something in his hand. A long, straight combat knife. Black handle. Wickedly clean.

He held it out to me, handle-first.

I stared.

"For when they get close," he said. "And they *will* get close."

My hand closed around it, feeling its weight. Real. Cold. Final.

I swallowed. "I've never used one."

"Pointy end goes in the dead guy," CJ offered flatly.

"Thanks. That clears it up."

"Don't thank me 'til you've tried it."

Despite the horror, I let out a breath that was dangerously close to a laugh. God help me, this family found ways to pull the edge off even the end of the world.

Sheila tapped the map again, now marked with her own notations in red Sharpie.

"We're about twenty-five miles from the extraction zone. Southeast. If this map's still accurate, we can follow the old canal road."

"Twenty-five miles," I repeated, already aching from the weight of the day. "On foot?"

"Yup," CJ said, shouldering his pack. "Through a hellhole."

"But the good news," Sheila added, "is the hardware store—the stash the survivors marked—is along that same route. A half-mile detour, tops. If the building's intact, we resupply. If not… we improvise."

Charles nodded. "We move quiet. Straight through back alleys. No direct streets unless necessary."

"And if we get cornered?" Shaun asked.

Charles locked eyes with him. "Then we get creative."

As we made our way down the stairs and out into the alley again, there was a stillness that wasn't comforting. It was *watchful.* I couldn't shake the feeling that the infected weren't just *wandering* anymore.

They were *lurking.*

Waiting.

I leaned close to Sheila as we jogged low along a rusted fence line. "Is it just me, or… are they moving differently?"

She didn't answer right away. Then:

"I've been noticing too. They're not smarter… not exactly. But they're not brainless. There's a… rhythm. Like pack behavior. You see one? There's always more close. And if you make noise—"

"—They converge," CJ finished from up ahead. "I've been watching them too. Some circle. Some wait. They're not chasing every noise like rabid dogs anymore."

"Mob mentality," Sheila said. "They're reacting to movement. Patterns."

"Some kind of primitive coordination," Shaun added. "Not planning, but reacting *together*. Not random."

Charles looked back at us mid-step. "We need to stop thinking of them as stupid. Desperate doesn't mean dumb."

That hit me harder than I expected. I had seen them tear through fences, chew through bone like it was soft bread—but even that terror was rooted in the comfort that they were *less* than us. Monsters. Mindless.

But if they *weren't*?

If they could *learn*?

"What happens if they start working together?" I asked.

No one answered.

Because we were already seeing what that looked like.

And it was only getting worse.

We reached the hardware store by dusk.

The building stood like a battered husk, its front collapsed inward under the weight of some long-dead vehicle. We circled to the side, stepping carefully over broken glass and busted concrete. Not a sound but the crunch of our boots and the whisper of wind through jagged metal.

Shaun took point, his rifle up and body low. "Clear so far."

CJ crouched beside the side door, tools in hand. "Locked. Give me ten seconds."

"I'll give you five," Charles muttered, back to the wall.

"Great. Pressure makes me faster."

"Pressure makes you dead," Shaun added flatly.

CJ smirked, twisted something, and with a click, the door opened.

We slipped inside, single file, rifles sweeping every corner. Rows of collapsed shelves greeted us—rusted tools, splintered crates, and a faint, putrid smell rising from somewhere deep in the back.

Then I heard it. A sound I hadn't heard before.

Scrape… tap… scrape…

Something quick. Too quick.

Shaun froze. "Did you hear that?"

Before anyone could respond, it hit.

A blur of movement crashed through the shelves, a flash of grey skin and gnarled muscle—inhumanly fast. The air cracked as metal bent under its momentum.

It launched straight for Sheila.

"NO—!" I yelled, instinct taking over.

I raised the pistol—sight barely aligned—fired.

The first round missed.

The second didn't.

The bullet struck its shoulder, just enough to jolt its trajectory. Sheila ducked as it soared over her and crashed into the wall, splinters flying. Shaun was already on it, rifle barking as he closed the distance.

"IT'S A RUNNER!" he yelled.

The thing scrambled upright, howling—its jaw split too wide, nearly unhinged. The eyes weren't cloudy like the others. They were black, hateful. *Aware.*

CJ flanked from the left. "Shoot, now!"

Charles fired twice. Shaun emptied a mag into its back. The creature didn't fall—it *twitched*, staggered, tried to lunge again—

—but then Sheila, of all people, ran forward and jammed a crowbar straight through its side, anchoring it for just a second.

One last shot from Charles—directly through the skull.

It collapsed, convulsing, then went still.

The silence that followed was too loud.

"That," CJ said, panting, "was not a normal biter."

"Fast," Shaun said, reloading. "Too fast."

"Muscle mass was different," Sheila added, wiping blood from her cheek. "Almost… engineered."

"We'll classify that as a 'Sprinter,'" CJ muttered. "Y'know. For when we write the survival guide none of us will live to finish."

"Still alive," Charles barked. "Keep it tight. That noise drew others."

He was right.

In less than thirty seconds, they were on us.

Screams tore from the darkness. Glass shattered. Dozens of them—biters—poured through the front and side like a flood, eyes wild, jaws snapping.

"DEFENSIVE FORMATION!" Charles shouted. "KEEP THE PACKAGE CENTERED!"

That was me. *The package.*

I hit the ground behind a shelf as Echo Black opened fire—bullets ripping through skulls, limbs, walls. Shaun moved like a blade, carving a path with his rifle and switching to a knife when they closed in. CJ covered the right side, hot-wiring a nail gun and firing steel into skulls with a cackle that bordered on unhinged.

"God, I missed hardware stores!"

Charles slammed a broken pipe into one biter's gut and fired point-blank into its skull. Sheila ducked behind a counter, snapping shots and tossing a small propane canister down the aisle.

"SHAUN!"

"ON IT!"

He fired.

BOOM.

Smoke and gore erupted.

Still, they came.

The bodies piled around us like sandbags, but the family didn't falter—not for a second. They weren't just fighting. They were *reading each other*, moving in sync, like one deadly organism built for war.

Then it was over.

Breathing heavy. Blood dripping. Silence returned—this time like an omen, not a relief.

Charles leaned against a shelf, chest rising and falling. "Anyone hit?"

"No," Shaun said. "Close, but no."

"Still vertical," CJ muttered, wiping blood from his face.

Sheila looked at me.

"You okay?" she asked.

I nodded slowly, then glanced at the downed sprinter.

"What the hell was that thing?"

"No idea," she said.

"But it won't be the last."

We moved deeper into the store, weapons ready, every footstep muffled by ash and glass.

The backroom was supposed to be the stash. A steel-reinforced shipping container tucked behind the inventory cages. CJ unlatched the dented padlock while Sheila checked for movement outside.

The door creaked open with a metallic groan.

What we found inside wasn't hope.

It was history.

Blood painted the walls in arcs and handprints. Shell casings carpeted the floor. Shattered crates lay toppled, contents long looted—or used.

CJ crouched over a pile of torn cardboard labeled "5.56 NATO" and held up one of the boxes.

"Empty."

He tossed it aside, moved to the next. "Empty."

He kicked a larger bin. "Empty, empty, *goddamn EMPTY!*"

Only a couple of plastic water bottles remained, half-frozen and coated in dried gore. Shaun handed one to me without a word, then took the other for himself.

It felt wrong, drinking from something someone else may have died holding.

Charles didn't say anything. He just stood there, scanning the walls. His silence said enough.

A rusted cot was tucked into the corner. Blood pooled underneath.

Carved into the wall beside it were four words, scratched deep with something sharp:

"IT LEARNS. IT WAITS."

I stared at the message. It looked frantic, dug in with such force that it bent the metal around each word.

CJ swallowed hard. "They tried. You can see it… they really tried to hold out."

Sheila touched the cot gently, her voice quiet. "They didn't just die here. They were *slaughtered*."

"We're not staying long," Charles said, finally. "Drink, breathe, and get moving."

"We're 24 miles out," Sheila confirmed, eyes on the map. "We'll need to cover more ground before night fully falls."

That's when we heard it.

Boom.

A single, heavy footstep.

The floor *shuddered*.

We froze.

BOOM.

Again—closer.

CJ raised his rifle slowly. "That's not thunder."

The back wall groaned, shelves rattling.

Then—through a massive hole torn through the outer structure—it emerged.

A giant.

Eight feet tall, maybe more. Muscles bulging unnaturally under torn, grey flesh. Its skull was misshapen, as if cracked and fused together again in all the wrong places. A patchwork of thick veins throbbed across its arms and neck. Black drool oozed from its mouth.

Its left arm was barely an arm at all—more like a slab of bone, sharpened and serrated.

Its right hand still gripped a twisted hunk of metal.

The rotors from our helicopter.

My blood froze.

Charles's voice was a whisper. "That's the bastard that grounded us."

The thing stared at us—no charge, no roar, just... watched like it *remembered.*

Then it raised the rotor in one hand and *screamed.*

The shelves around us shattered from the force of it.

And just like that, the sprinting stopped.

Charles raised his rifle. "MOVE. NOW."

NO WAY BUT THROUGH

We ran.

No formation. No strategy. Just instinct. Movement. Survival.

The behemoth behind us roared, shattering windows and rattling street signs as it tore through the building we'd just escaped. Chunks of brick and twisted steel rained down around us. The tremors from its steps made my teeth chatter.

Echo Black moved with terrifying purpose. Even while low on ammo, they didn't waste a single round.

"DON'T SHOOT IT!" Charles barked. "It won't stop!"

We vaulted through a broken fence, spilled into the alley beyond. Blood smeared the brick walls on either side. The sky was blackening—sunset disappearing beneath the ash and smoke curling from distant fires.

"Status!" Charles yelled.

"Two mags!" CJ replied.

"Half a mag!" Shaun added. "And that's being generous."

"I'm dry!" Sheila called. "Knife and sidearm only."

"I have three rounds," I said, breath ragged.

They didn't answer. No time.

More infected flooded in behind the behemoth. Dozens. Then more. We were being *driven*. Herded. The mob was no longer mindless—it moved like something *controlled it*. Channeled it.

The family didn't panic. But they were strained. I could see it.

Sheila suddenly ducked into a side alley, grabbing my arm and yanking me with her.

"This way!" she hissed.

Charles pivoted without hesitation. "You sure?!"

"I know these streets," she shot back. "This was a containment zone—they used barricades and redirected routes. I can get us out of the funnel!"

We weaved through the debris-strewn corridors of the city. Graffiti-covered walls. Burnt-out storefronts. Scattered bodies. The air reeked of copper and rot.

Every turn Sheila made seemed impossible, and yet it worked—keeping us one step ahead at least for now.

"Dead end," CJ warned at one turn.

"No," Sheila whispered, pressing her hand against the wall. She scanned the base of a crumbled maintenance tunnel and kicked through the trash until her fingers found what she was looking for—an old maintenance hatch.

"Ventilation access. From the quarantine days. Cuts through three blocks underground."

Shaun didn't wait. He pried the hatch open. "Move, *now*."

We crawled through the narrow, filthy tunnel. Rats. Piss. Blood-streaked handprints smeared on the walls. The stench was overwhelming. I nearly vomited.

Sheila stayed behind me, guiding me with calm but urgent precision.

"Left here. Drop down. Careful—pipe's loose."

Boom.

The roar came again—above us. The tunnel quaked. Dust and rubble fell.

"Sheila!" Charles called from the front. "We've got a breach—move it!"

She motioned for me to crawl faster. "GO, Hector. Don't stop."

We emerged into an old maintenance substation—dark, silent. Shafts of light pierced through cracked concrete above. CJ moved to secure the exits while Shaun pushed a storage crate in front of the vent we just came from.

Charles sat against the wall, gasping, checking his mags. "I've got six rounds. That's it."

"Four," Shaun muttered. "And a blade."

"I've got one magazine," CJ said, holding it up. "Half full. Maybe."

Sheila sat beside me and whispered, "We've got two options: bleed to death slowly, or run dry swinging."

"What about the extraction?" I asked.

"We keep moving. Twenty-three miles now. One click at a time."

Shaun was the first to his feet. "Then we don't stop."

But then we heard the sound again—farther off, but not far enough.

A deep, thunderous breathing.

It hadn't lost us.

And it wasn't alone.

Sheila stood, eyes scanning the shadows. Then she pointed to a faded street map plastered on the wall, torn but legible. Her fingers traced a route in silence.

"There," she said. "If we cut through the old metro line, we bypass the main streets. It's dangerous. But we'll lose the herd."

"And the big one?" CJ asked quietly.

She looked at him with fire in her eyes. "We keep moving. And we pray it's not waiting."

No one spoke after that.

We tightened our gear, checked our knives. There was nothing left to joke about. Just a single direction left:

Forward.

The metro tunnel swallowed us whole.

It was pitch black.

The kind of darkness that felt *alive*—coiling, breathing. My flashlight barely cut through the black. Dust particles danced in the beam like snow in a broken world. The air was thick with mildew, oil, and something *rotting*.

Water dripped somewhere in the distance. A slow, rhythmic beat. *Plink... plink... plink...*

The silence wasn't empty—it was *crowded*.

It felt like the walls were listening.

Shaun took point, moving slowly but deliberately. His knife gleamed in the faint light as he swept it like a surgeon, clearing corners before we passed. CJ was just behind, eyes darting, one hand on my shoulder, guiding me forward without a word.

Charles whispered, "No gunfire unless we're out of options."

Sheila nodded, her eyes never leaving the map in her hands. "This line should intersect with the Lexington exit in half a mile. If the old service ladder's intact, we'll be above ground again."

I stepped into something wet. Sticky. Thick. I didn't ask what it was.

CJ muttered under his breath, just loud enough to be heard, "Feels like we're being watched."

We stopped.

Silence.

But then—*scrape.*

Far down the tunnel. Metal against stone. A dragging sound.

Everyone froze.

Charles raised his fist in a silent signal to hold.

Then came a soft, subtle *breathing* sound. Not close. But not far.

Sheila crouched beside a rusted support beam, flashlight angled down to avoid glare.

Shaun whispered, "We've got movement."

CJ was calmer. "Multiple echoes. Three sets, maybe four. Close together. Not charging. Not... normal."

The breathing grew faint, then faded.

Gone.

Or hiding.

Sheila's voice was low, but clear. "They're adapting."

"They always do," Charles said.

I swallowed hard. "What now?"

They all looked to Sheila.

She didn't answer right away. She just studied the darkness ahead, listening.

Then she stood slowly, finally answering. "Now? Now we walk quiet, watch each other's backs, and pretend we've still got time."

We moved again—deeper.

The tunnel curved left. Around the bend, we found a collapsed subway car. Rusted. Empty. Its windows were smashed. Something dark was smeared along the ceiling inside.

CJ ran a hand across a dent in the side. "Something hit this from the outside. Hard."

Sheila examined the impact point. "Pressure split inward. Whatever it was, it *threw* something heavy. Or it *was* something heavy."

Charles didn't wait. "No sightseeing. Keep it tight."

Suddenly—*SCREEEEECH.*

A metallic wail behind us.

We spun.

The flashlight bounced wildly off the walls.

Nothing.

Just black.

Then the sound again—but closer.

CJ raised his rifle, shaking his head. "They're hunting. With sound. They want us to panic."

"I don't panic," Shaun muttered.

"Liar," CJ whispered back.

It was the first joke I'd heard in over an hour, but no one laughed.

We crept through the final length of the tunnel. Every step screamed through the silence. Every breath felt borrowed.

The exit ladder came into view—bent but intact.

Sheila climbed first, checking above. "Clear."

One by one, we ascended.

And as I stepped onto the surface again, blinking under the faint twilight glow above the city ruins, I realized something terrifying:

The silence hadn't followed us.

The tunnel below stayed dark.

But something *in it*... still watched.

And it *knew our scent now.*

THE LONG WAY AROUND

The streets were quieter now.

Not safe. Not even close. But quieter.

That's how you knew the worst had already happened — not because the noise stopped, but because no one was left to make it.

We moved in silence. Not out of strategy anymore — just preservation. There was nothing left to say.

The neighborhood we entered had once been upscale. Glass towers cracked like porcelain teapots, cars rusted in perfect parking spots, homes left mid-breakfast. A child's toy tricycle still stood on the sidewalk. No blood nearby. Just... abandoned.

Shaun walked point, M4 raised, barrel twitching with every shadow. CJ stayed behind me, watching the rear, his expression unreadable. Charles took a flank, knife already in hand. Sheila led.

She didn't speak. Just moved.

The map was gone. Lost in the chaos when the tunnel collapsed behind us. Now she relied on memory — counting streets, watching signs, scanning landmarks that were barely recognizable anymore.

She was the only reason we still had direction.

We cleared another block.

No infected. No movement. Just heat and silence.

Sheila stopped near the twisted remains of a burned-out convenience store. She raised a hand. "This was marked as a stash point."

"Marked when?" CJ muttered. "The world's changed since Tuesday."

"It's still worth checking," she replied flatly.

Charles didn't argue. He kicked the door in, and we swept in formation.

Rotten food. Ransacked shelves. Blood dried to a rusty brown under our boots.

No water.

No ammo.

Not even a bandage.

Just flies.

CJ ripped open the freezer door and swore under his breath. Empty. Still cold, somehow, but empty.

Shaun checked behind the counter. "Not even painkillers."

Sheila shook her head. "We're six miles off-route. This stash was our best shot at regrouping. Closest next marker is another three miles."

I could see the frustration in her eyes.

She blamed herself.

She shouldn't have.

"This isn't on you," I said quietly.

She glanced at me but didn't reply.

Outside, the sky darkened. Not night — just a storm pushing smoke and ash across the rooftops. Visibility dropped fast.

Charles checked his rifle. "Two mags left."

Shaun popped his. "One full, one partial."

CJ just shook his head. "You don't want to know."

I looked down at the pistol they'd given me. Only five rounds left.

I didn't ask if I'd get more.

Because we were out.

Of everything.

We moved cautiously, weaving between burnt-out cars and collapsed storefronts. The silence was thicker than smoke, like the whole world was holding its breath.

Then, CJ broke it — like he always did.

"You know," he said casually, "if we find a Costco, I'm looting every rotisserie chicken they ever made. Don't even care if it's fossilized. I miss flavor."

Charles, without missing a beat: "You didn't even season your food before the world ended."

"That's a lie," CJ said. "I once used paprika."

Shaun snorted. "You used *ketchup* and called it spicy."

"I was experimenting with fusion cuisine."

Sheila muttered, "Fusion between what, regret and disappointment?"

Even I laughed — a real, involuntary bark of amusement.

CJ grinned. "See? President gets it. Man appreciates a fine meal and a trash palate."

"I'd kill for trash palate," I admitted, still smiling. "Even stale pretzels would feel like a banquet right now."

As the group quieted again, I pulled the photo from my pocket. It was worn, edges frayed from too many touches. Emma. Blonde hair, giant smile, standing in front of a glitter-covered volcano with the words *Boom Science!* barely visible behind her.

CJ glanced over my shoulder. "That her?"

"Yeah," I said. "My daughter. Ten years old. Smart. Loud. Brave as hell."

"Looks like she'd be running this squad by now," he said.

"She probably would," I replied. "She kept me grounded. Even now... she still does."

Shaun leaned in. "Still in a safe zone?"

"Last I heard. Near Denver. It's been quiet since."

Charles gave me a firm nod. "You're getting back to her. That's the only direction we're moving."

I looked at him, at all of them. This family I didn't know a week ago, but now I couldn't imagine walking without.

Sheila smiled faintly. "You're lucky. Most people didn't get anyone."

CJ pointed to himself. "Yeah, he gets the apocalypse escort package with built-in dysfunctional humor and tactical support. That's like the zombie VIP pass."

Shaun grumbled, "We should charge hourly."

Charles muttered, "He's not tipping, I guarantee it."

The laugh that followed wasn't loud. It was tired, cracked — but honest. And in that moment, it gave me more strength than a whole armory ever could.

We kept walking. And I held the photo just a little tighter.

The air was colder now. Not because the temperature dropped — though it might have — but because something in the wind felt *off*. Like it knew.

We moved through a shattered alleyway, boots crunching broken glass. The sun had dipped low enough to paint everything in a burnt-orange hue. Shadows grew long. The world felt like it was fading.

Sheila stopped, flattening herself against the wall. She pulled out some paper from her vest and crouched down, and started drawing a map from memory. Her voice was steady.

"We're still fifteen miles from the extraction zone. Looks like Greene Street's collapse cut off one of our backup paths."

CJ leaned down beside her, watching closely.

"Okay," she said, pointing with the edge of her knife. "If we wrap around east toward Lexington, we can follow that broken tram line until it spits us out near the highway. That'll cut through this zone here — Sector Six-B."

CJ nodded. "The same sector that had the chemical plant?"

"Yeah," Sheila answered. "The blast radius stopped most of the infected from clustering, but it's not empty. We'll need to go silent. Fast and tight."

CJ scanned it again. "So, we cut throug here, avoid this pileup, and hit the freeway?"

Sheila locked eyes with him. "Exactly. You remember that. If something happens to me—"

"Stop," CJ said, a little too sharp.

She didn't flinch. "Just in case. You need to know the route."

He held her gaze. Then, reluctantly, nodded. "I got it."

She handed the map to him. He stuffed it into his vest.

Shaun swept past, checking corners. "We're still clear. For now."

Charles adjusted his grip on his rifle. "Good. We keep moving. Double file. Quiet. If they're hunting, we're not gonna give them a scent."

I checked my magazine again. Four rounds. Four chances. Maybe less if I missed. I felt the knife Shaun gave me shift in my waistband. The metal was cold against my skin — a reminder that if things went bad, I wouldn't go down helpless.

We stepped back onto the street, Sheila falling in beside me as we moved.

"How's your breathing?" she asked, not looking at me.

"Controlled. But every time I blink, I see that crash again."

"That's normal," she replied. "Just don't blink too long."

She didn't smile. None of us did. There wasn't space for it anymore.

We crossed the street and slipped into another alley, darker now — tighter. The smell of rot returned, heavier than before. Something was watching. We all felt it.

Shaun tensed. "Eyes open."

Something ahead groaned. Something huge.

And the wind shifted again — wrong.

But none of us knew.

None of us could've guessed.

Not yet.

The tunnel was quiet. Too quiet.

Our boots echoed through the damp underground, the water around our soles reflecting the flickering beams of our flashlights. It smelled like rust and rot. Pipes moaned above us. Every few feet, we stepped around dried blood or smeared handprints fading into old grime.

But nothing moved.

CJ gave a nervous chuckle. "It's like a haunted house without the overpriced tickets."

Even Shaun cracked a faint smile. "Or the corn dogs."

Charles snorted. "I'd kill for a damn corn dog."

We let that silence return. For once, it wasn't suffocating. Just… still.

Sheila was leading, laser-focused, marking the route in her head. She walked tall, steady, alert — like nothing could touch her. Like she'd seen everything this world had to throw.

She never even saw it coming.

It came from the shadows without a sound.

One second, she was walking — the next, a massive arm exploded from a rusted service duct to her left and hooked her around the waist like a rag doll.

Her scream tore through the tunnel — not a short cry. A long, agonizing one. High-pitched and primal.

We turned, too late.

The abomination dragged her halfway into the wall cavity before we even saw its face. It was barely human—a massive, misshapen thing, split open across the jaw, skin stretched taut over bone and muscle, one eye hanging loose and swinging as it bit down on her shoulder like tearing into meat.

Sheila screamed again — louder this time, writhing, fighting — blood gushing down her arm, her legs kicking hard enough to dent the pipe she hit.

"SHEILA!" Charles roared, already moving.

CJ was frozen. Shaun was screaming. I raised my gun and fired three wild shots into the dark. One clipped it, I think — but it didn't even flinch.

"GET HER OUT!" I yelled.

Shaun lunged forward, grabbed her boot — and for half a second, we all thought we had her.

But then it bit again, deep into her lower back. The sound was wet, horrible, the kind of thing you can't forget even if you try.

She didn't scream this time.

Her head lolled forward. Blood spilled from her mouth.

Charles unloaded his entire mag. Screaming. Blind. Furious.

The monster let go. Sheila's body dropped like trash, hitting the tunnel floor with a lifeless thud.

We all rushed to her.

CJ was shaking her. "Mom—Mom—please—no no no no no—!"

Charles dropped to his knees. Shaun was sobbing and cursing, punching the wall like it would bleed for him.

I stood frozen. I wanted to move. I wanted to help.

But all I could do was stare at her empty eyes.

Still open. Still staring at nothing.

We'd survived the crash. The streets. The tunnel.

And now…

We were only 15 miles from extraction.

And Sheila Sanders — Bacon One — was gone.

DEAD RECKONING

None of us moved at first.

The tunnel was silent except for the quiet sound of CJ's sobbing, mixed with Shaun's shallow, panicked breaths. Their weapons hung useless at their sides, their bodies slumped around her like they could shield her from what had already happened.

But Sheila wasn't there anymore.

Only the body remained—broken, limp, blood still leaking out of her onto the wet concrete. Her face was peaceful in a way that made it worse.

Charles knelt beside her. His thick hands were trembling. Not from fear. From heartbreak. I could see it in the way he avoided her eyes, like if he looked, it would all be real.

His fingers slowly reached for her neck and unclipped the thin chain of her dog tags. The metal glinted faintly in the tunnel's dim light, smudged with blood.

He didn't say a word.

He pulled his own tags from under his shirt and clipped hers onto his. The soft clink of metal on metal echoed louder than it should've in that narrow space.

Then his breath caught. He leaned in, brushing a hand against her cheek—his thumb gently wiping away blood, as if she might stir from it.

"Sheila…" he whispered. His voice cracked, and the rest barely made it out. "I should've protected you. I promised I'd keep you safe…"

He bowed his head, forehead resting lightly against hers.

"You were the heart of this family. You held us together. You kept me sane," he murmured. "I don't know how to do this without you. I don't even want to."

CJ stepped closer, his voice small and trembling. "Dad…"

Shaun was quiet, but when he finally spoke, it was barely above a whisper. "She's gone, Dad."

That shattered him.

Charles's shoulders collapsed inward as he let out a soft, choked sob. He reached out and cradled her face in both hands like it was something fragile and precious.
 "I know," he said, barely holding it together.
 He kissed her forehead and lingered there, breathing her in one last time.

CJ knelt beside him, tears flowing freely. "We love you, Mom…"

"I'm sorry I didn't react fast enough," Shaun said, stepping to the other side. "But we have to finish this… for her."

Charles looked between them, his eyes raw, red, and full of everything he couldn't say.

He nodded slowly, brushing one last strand of hair from her face with trembling fingers.

CJ wiped at his face with the back of his hand, but it was useless. His lips were shaking.

"She was… she was the map," he muttered. "She was everything…"

Shaun didn't speak. He sat with his back against the tunnel wall, staring at the body, his rifle across his lap. His jaw was clenched so tight it looked like it might break. His eyes were glassy and red, like he wasn't fully there anymore.

"I'm sorry," I whispered. I didn't know what else to say. I wasn't sure anything would've mattered.

Charles slowly stood. Not tall, not strong—just a man trying to hold the pieces of himself together.
He turned to CJ. His voice cracked. "You remember the route?"

CJ nodded, still crying. "Yeah. Yeah, she showed me. I got it. I just…"

"I know," Charles said. He put a hand on CJ's shoulder. "But you have to lead now."

CJ swallowed hard and stood up. "Fourteen miles," he whispered. "We can do it. For her."

Shaun spoke, his voice low and cold. "We're burning daylight."
He stood. Turned away from her body.
But he didn't look back.
None of us did.

We left her there in the tunnel. We had to.

Not because we wanted to.

Because we didn't have a choice.

We walked.

No one spoke.

The only sounds were our boots against broken pavement and the distant moans of the dead echoing through the city's hollow bones.

CJ took point. It was strange seeing him lead. His stride was steady, but his head tilted often, always checking the map, always second-guessing. You could see the hesitation with every stop. Sheila used to lead like she could see through the buildings. CJ was trying to walk in her shadow.

Charles followed behind him, not far, watching like a ghost—rifle held low, eyes scanning the rooftops but not really seeing them. The man had always seemed invincible to me. Now, he looked like a wreck barely held together by gunpowder and grief.

Shaun was the rear guard, like always. But there was something different about him. He walked slower. Head lower. He didn't correct CJ when he missed a turn. He didn't even grunt. His silence was louder than any scream he'd ever let out.

And me?

I stayed in the middle, clutching my rifle like it meant something. I kept hearing her scream.

Kept seeing Charles clip her tags to his own.

Kept wondering how this world could steal people that quickly. That cruelly.

CJ stopped us a few blocks later. We ducked into a burned-out diner—no windows, no signs of life. Just the smell of old grease and scorched flesh.

He crouched behind the counter, pulled the torn map from his jacket, and spread it across the grime-covered surface.

"We're here," he said, voice rough. He pointed with a shaking finger. "Extraction's northeast, thirteen miles—if we keep tight and quiet, skirt the edge of Sector Eight, we can get there by nightfall. But…"

He looked up at Charles.

"The next few blocks are hot. Real hot. I saw nests on the rooftops when we passed the church."

"Then we don't go loud unless we have to," Charles said, voice distant. "Sheila wouldn't have."

CJ nodded.

Shaun checked his mags in silence. He didn't look at the map. Didn't need to.

Charles stepped beside CJ and looked down at the torn, bloodstained paper.

"She showed you the whole path?"

CJ met his eyes and, for a second, that same sarcastic glint returned.

"She made me memorize it," he said. "Like a damn quiz. I got this."

Charles didn't smile.

But he nodded.

"We follow you, then."

CJ looked like he wanted to say something more, but he just folded the map again. His hands lingered on it like he was afraid it might crumble if he let go too fast.

We stepped out of the diner back into the street.

One down.

Three to go.

And the world around us hadn't changed.

But we had.

We should've seen it sooner.

The wind shifted first—thick with rot, like something ancient crawling out of the earth. The groans were louder now. Closer. More unified. They weren't wandering… they were converging.

CJ froze mid-step and turned.

"Oh no…"

It dropped from a roof like a sack of meat and nightmares—thirty feet in the air, landed on a parked car, and crushed it flat in a single, echoing *crunch*.

The monster that killed Sheila.

Twisted. Bigger than before. Covered in scars from the crash, but moving like it felt nothing.

Six glowing eyes blinked out of sync.

Its shoulders rolled forward like it was stretching before a feast.

And behind it…

An entire street of infected poured in behind us—fast, crawling, snarling like they were being pulled by something unseen.

Charles froze.

Just for a second.

Just for a *second*.

His rifle dipped. His eyes locked on that thing—on what it had taken. He didn't move.

Didn't speak.

CJ saw it too. His scream broke the paralysis.

"Dad—MOVE!"

Shaun yanked Charles sideways as the beast roared and sprinted forward like a freight train. Bullets lit up the air—CJ and Shaun unleashing hell. I fired too, but it wasn't enough. It never was.

The horde surged with it.

And then it was chaos.

CJ dove into the crowd, blade in one hand, pistol in the other, yelling like a madman. Shaun was surgical—rifle controlled bursts, switching to his knife the moment they got close. Charles stumbled at first—his hands shaking, aim off—until one infected slammed into him and knocked him flat.

He didn't fight back.

He didn't even raise his arm.

I saw it in real time—he was done. The fire in him was out. Gone.

"CHARLES!" I shouted, emptying a mag into a crawler trying to reach him.

No response.

I ran. Without thinking. Without a plan. I grabbed the butt of my pistol and slammed it into the skull of a twitching corpse at his feet.

"GET UP!" I screamed.

Still nothing.

CJ kicked a screamer off his back and ran over. "We need you, Dad! NOW!"

Still nothing.

So I did the only thing I could think of.

I slapped him.

Hard.

His head jerked sideways. His eyes snapped into focus.

"You want her death to mean NOTHING?" I shouted. "Then stay down."

He blinked. And then the switch flipped.

Charles roared—a sound like the world cracking—and lunged to his feet, grabbing his rifle like it was part of him again.

The beast was coming back.

He aimed.

So did CJ.

So did Shaun.

So did I.

And together, we *unloaded.* Every last round. Every scream. Every bit of grief and hatred and horror, all pouring out of the barrel like fire.

The thing took hits—stumbled—roared back.

CJ leapt and drove a knife into its side, screaming.

Shaun slid between its legs and fired upward into its gut.

Charles tackled it from behind.

And I—

I ran up with my pistol, blood coating my hands, and pulled the trigger into its temple.

Click.

Empty.

The beast roared one last time—staggered—slammed against a wall—and finally dropped.

Dead.

The street was a graveyard. Bodies. Blood. Smoke.

All of us stood there, panting, covered in gore. Guns empty. Eyes hollow.

CJ was leaning on his knees, muttering "Mom" under his breath.

Shaun sat on the curb, covered in blood not his own.

Charles walked to me slowly.

And then—

He nodded.

Not a thank you.

Not an apology.

Just a look that said: *I'm here now.*

And we kept moving.

We heard it before we saw it.

A scream.

Not one of terror.

But raw, unfiltered defiance.

"COME ON! IS THAT ALL YOU GOT?! I'M RIGHT HERE, YOU SONS OF—!"

We turned the corner—and time stopped.

There were dozens of them.

A full street is swallowed by the infected. Biters clawing over wrecked cars and bodies. The mystery man stood in the middle, surrounded on all sides—shirt shredded, a blood-covered steel pipe in both hands, swinging like a madman just to stay alive.

He was already bleeding from a gash above his brow, one eye swollen nearly shut—but his roars cut through the chaos like a battle cry.

Shaun said nothing. He charged.

Charles was right behind him.

CJ glanced at me, then sprinted.

And I ran too.

We hit the horde like a thunderclap.

CJ tackled one off the guys back, knife slamming into its temple with a sickening *crunch*. Another turned on him—Shaun grabbed its head and twisted, snapping its neck with a roar. The mystery man caught sight of them and howled in relief, crushing a biter's skull beneath his boot.

"DON'T YOU DIE ON ME!" Charles screamed, slashing through two more. "NONE OF YOU!"

The horde surged.

We were swallowed by a wave of limbs, teeth, and blood.

I felt something grab my shoulder—I turned and stabbed, blindly, into its face. Another knocked me down. I kicked it off just in time for CJ to drag me back to my feet.

"Don't stop moving, Hector!" he shouted. "You stop, you die!"

Shaun screamed behind us. Three biters had him pinned—the mystery guy shoulder-checked one so hard its spine bent backward. Charles grabbed the other two and drove his knife into both in a single brutal motion, muscles shaking.

"WHERE'S YOUR GUN?!" Charles barked.

"Empty!" CJ yelled back. "All of us are!"

Only blades now.

And fists.

And fury.

Blood sprayed.

Arms flailed.

Knives punched into bone and didn't come out clean.

Shaun was limping, bleeding from his arm. CJ had a bite on his vest—thank God for armor. The mystery man got cut across the ribs and barely flinched. Charles took a hit to the shoulder but didn't even slow down.

We were back-to-back. Slashing. Stabbing. Screaming.

They didn't stop coming.

The mystery guy shoved me behind him and grabbed a fire extinguisher off a wreck—he used it like a hammer, bashing skulls with animalistic rage.

CJ tackled an infected off Charles and stabbed it through the eye.

Shaun got knocked down again—this time, I pulled him back and planted my knife into the infected's throat before it could sink its teeth in.

"GET UP!" I screamed. "WE'RE NOT DONE YET!"

We formed a tight circle, backs to each other, dripping with sweat and blood, surrounded by twitching bodies and staggering monsters.

And then—

Silence.

We were shaking.

Panting.

But still standing.

The mystery guy spit blood onto the pavement and wiped his mouth.

"That all of 'em?" he rasped, breathing fire.

CJ doubled over, coughing. "No... but they're dead enough for now."

Charles looked around like he was still in the fight, chest rising like a war drum. Blood dripped off his chin. His eyes burned.

"You good?" he growled at the mystery man.

"No," he said, smiling like a savage. "But I'm alive."

Charles stared a beat longer—then stepped forward.

"Viper Two," he said. "You're with us."

The man took his hand and nodded, panting.

"Name's Bryan."

7

SCARS AND SHADOWS

The air still stank of blood and sweat.

But Bryan—he walked through the aftermath like a man who'd just won a championship fight.

Broad shoulders squared, pipe slung over one shoulder like a bat, a bloodied grin spread across his face.

"Now *that's* what I call cardio," he said with a chuckle, glancing at Shaun and CJ, who were both leaning against the wall, catching their breath.

Shaun gave a dry, exhausted laugh. "You do this for fun?"

"Nope," Bryan said, stretching out his neck. "I do this for my girls."

CJ raised an eyebrow. "Girls?"

Bryan reached into the inner pocket of his shredded jacket and carefully pulled out a crumpled, laminated photo. It was torn at the corners, blood-specked, but intact. He held it out, reverently, like a relic.

"My wife, Mel. And those two little firecrackers are Karen and Emma. Ten and seven," he said, his voice shifting—still deep, still steady, but quieter now. "Last time I saw them, they were being evacuated toward the inner wall near Brookline. We got separated in the chaos. I've been moving ever since."

I leaned in and studied the photo. His wife, tall and elegant, smiled in the center with her arms wrapped around two laughing girls. One had her father's eyes. The other is his unstoppable grin.

Charles stepped forward and looked without saying a word. Then he nodded.

"We'll find them," he said firmly. "You fight like hell for them. Keep doing that. You're one of us now."

"Damn right he is," CJ said, nudging Shaun. "Saves our asses and brings morale? I'm gonna start calling him Captain Comeback."

Shaun smirked through his bloodied lip. "Keep talkin' like that and he's gonna expect hugs."

Bryan chuckled, then gave them both a friendly clap on the shoulder—one that nearly knocked CJ sideways.

"Just remember," Bryan said, gesturing toward the corpses behind them, "that's what we leave behind. But *this*—" he tapped the photo once, "—this is what we live for."

I couldn't stop myself from thinking of Emma. My own photo is tucked safely in my vest. My daughter, ten years old, blonde, laughing in a summer dress the last time I saw her. The only reason I haven't completely broken is.

The silence afterward was different than before.

Less haunted.

A little warmer.

Like we still had something to fight for.

"Alright," Charles finally said. "Everyone, check your gear. We move in five. Still eleven miles from the extraction site, and we're out of second chances."

We were back on the move.

The blood on our hands hadn't dried, but we pushed forward—streets carved open with shell holes, smoke clawing up from the wreckage of whatever this neighborhood once was.

No birds. No engines.

Just our boots on shattered pavement, the moaning of distant infected, and the creak of our own exhaustion.

Bryan walked beside me, pipe resting across his shoulders like it belonged there.

After a while, he glanced around and said, "Alright... I gotta ask. Why the hell are you all out here in *this?*"

Charles didn't look back, just kept scanning ahead. "We're babysitting."

CJ added, "World's most high-stakes escort mission."

Shaun grunted. "The president's got the cure. We're the shield."

Bryan's eyebrows shot up. "*The* cure?"

I gave a small nod. "If I don't make it to the extraction zone... humanity's got no shot."

Bryan let out a low whistle. "Damn. No pressure, huh?"

"None at all," CJ muttered.

We turned down a twisted alley, taking a breather. Bryan leaned against the brick wall, pipe resting at his foot.

"So what's with the code names?" he asked. "You've all been calling each other stuff like Viper Two and Sparky Three. You guys G.I. Joe or something?"

Charles let out a tired, half-laugh. "We're Echo Black. Special Forces. Families don't usually get the call together—but we're not exactly usual."

Shaun spoke up. "Viper Two's my dad. He's the muscle and the mouth."

Charles shot him a glare but didn't argue.

CJ raised a hand. "Diablo Four. That's me. I fix things. Usually, before they blow up."

"I'm Sparky Three," Shaun added. "Frontline. I shoot first, second, and third. Ask questions never."

"Bacon One," Charles said, voice dropping. "My wife. Navigator. She…"
He paused, pain flashing behind his eyes. "She kept us alive longer than we had any right to be."

Bryan nodded solemnly. "Sorry, man. She sounded like the real deal."

"She was," CJ said quietly.

After a moment, Bryan stood tall and grinned. "Alright. So what about me? I get a cool codename too, or what?"

Charles sized him up, expression unreadable. "Well… what're you known for?"

Bryan scratched the back of his neck. "Uh… I mean, I used to work at a shoe store. They called me 'Stack'… because I could stack shoeboxes stupid fast. Not exactly Navy SEAL material, but hey."

There was silence for a beat.

Then, in perfect unison, Shaun and CJ deadpanned:

"Stack Five."

Bryan blinked. "Wait, what?"

CJ shrugged. "It's dumb enough to fit."

Shaun added, "Means you're officially in."

Bryan laughed. "Stack Five. Sounds like a gang of angry toddlers."

Charles smirked for the first time in hours. "Well, Stack, welcome to Echo Black. Don't get killed."

Bryan nodded solemnly. "Not until I find my girls."

We kept walking.
Less alone.
Still outnumbered—but now five instead of four.

And somehow… that felt like something.

We moved carefully, boots crunching over glass and gravel. The buildings on either side of us loomed like skeletons—burnt-out windows, graffiti, and bloodstains telling the story of a city that died screaming.

But amid all that rot, Bryan—Stack Five—kept talking. Not out of ignorance. Out of defiance.

"You know," he said, shifting the pipe over his shoulder, "I used to dream about opening my own shoe store. Classy place. Not one of those warehouse chains. I mean—marble floors, clean lighting, walls with sneakers so fresh they could make grown men cry."

CJ smirked. "So basically… a church for hypebeasts."

Bryan chuckled. "Damn right. With a couch shaped like a shoebox."

Shaun grunted. "You're already designing furniture for it?"

Bryan nodded proudly. "Of course. Vision's important. I didn't have a name yet, though. Nothing felt right. Something cool… simple… unforgettable."

Charles raised an eyebrow. "Soul Stack?"

We all paused.

CJ groaned. "God, that's terrible. I love it."

Bryan laughed out loud, his voice echoing between buildings. "I might actually steal that."

It was… nice.

A moment that didn't feel like the end of the world. Just five people walking and talking about shoes.

Then—

A scream.

It wasn't distant.

It wasn't vague.

It tore through the street like a knife to the gut.

Bryan's whole body froze.

We all turned our heads at once—shouts, fast footsteps, terror in the air.

Then:

"DADDY!"

Bryan dropped his pipe and ran. No hesitation. Just pure instinct.

"BRYAN!" Shaun barked, sprinting after him.

We followed, guns raised, blood going cold.
The scream had come from less than a block away.

Another one rang out—this one higher-pitched. A child.

"HELP US! PLEASE!"

Bryan's voice exploded from up ahead.

"KAREN! EMMA!"

I felt my stomach collapse.

He'd told us his daughters' names.

Emma.

Just like mine.

We rounded the corner, weapons up, hearts in our throats—no idea what we'd find.

But already, I could see one thing clearly:

This wasn't going to be a rescue.

It was going to be a war.

The screaming cut through the chaos like a blade.

High. Young. Terrified.

Bryan was gone before anyone could speak—just a blur of muscle and panic crashing through the horde, bellowing his daughter's name like thunder.

"Go!" Charles shouted. "Stay tight!"

We were already in motion—Shaun slashing a snarling biter off his flank, CJ gutting another and kicking it through a shattered window. I followed, heart in my throat, gripping the knife like it was my only lifeline.

We cut through bodies—too many to count. No ammo. No time. Blood splattered our faces. Every breath was rot and rage.

The screams led us to a house at the end of a wrecked street. The front door hung by a single hinge. Bryan was inside before it hit the floor.

We charged in after him.

And froze.

The living room looked like a war zone.

Furniture torn to splinters.

Blood pooled on the carpet.

Handprints smeared across the walls in frantic streaks.

A woman's body—Karen, we knew without asking—was twisted in a corner. Her face looked peaceful. Her chest had been torn open.

Bryan knelt beside her, trembling.

His hand gently brushed her cheek.

Then—

"Daddy…"

A whisper.

We all turned toward the rubble-strewn hallway.

There—barely visible beneath a toppled shelf and two mangled corpses—a small girl, wide-eyed, bloody, reaching out.

Bryan didn't hesitate.

He ripped the shelf off, tossing it like cardboard. He grabbed her, held her tight, sobbing into her hair.

"It's okay. I've got you. You're safe."

Her little arms wrapped around his neck.

"I knew you'd come…"

Then came the growl.

From the kitchen.

Not the low moan of the infected.

Something worse.

Something wet.

Something *wrong*.

A figure dragged itself into the room—taller than any human, hunched and deformed. Its arms were muscular but too long, dragging talon-like claws across the floor. Its face… if it had one… was stitched with jagged bone, eyes milky and twitching.

A new mutated. One we hadn't seen before.

And it was fast.

Bryan turned just in time to see it leap.

Shaun tackled it mid-air, both slamming into the wall with a sickening crunch. CJ dove in behind him, driving his blade into its ribs—once, twice, three times.

It *screeched*—a blood-curdling wail that shattered glass.

Bryan backed toward the corner, clutching his daughter, eyes wide with terror.

Then the creature flung Shaun aside like paper and turned— razor arm whipping out like a whip.

Bryan tried to shield his daughter.

But he was too slow.

The blade ripped clean through her body.

He stumbled backward—screaming, holding only her arm.

She was gone before she could scream again.

Blood-soaked Bryan's chest. Her tiny fingers twitched in his grasp, then went limp.

"No…" he whispered. "No, no, no—"

CJ and Shaun leapt back in, stabbing it over and over, their screams mixing with Bryan's sobs. Charles slammed his knife into its throat. I watched the light leave its eyes as it dropped, twitching on the floor.

But Bryan didn't move.

He dropped to his knees.

Clutching the arm like it was still part of her. Like if he held on tight enough, the rest of her would come back.

"I had her," he whispered. "I had her in my arms…"

The rest of us stood frozen, bloodied and breathless.

No one had anything to say.

What words could you possibly offer a man holding half his daughter?

I turned away.

Because I couldn't bear to look any longer.

And because I knew—

This world wasn't going to stop breaking us.

Bryan stood shaking, face soaked with sweat and blood, his daughter's limp arm still clutched in his hand. His eyes were wild—red, glassy, broken.

He turned to the sky and screamed.

"FUUUUUCK!"

The sound ripped through the air like a bomb, echoing off the ruined walls around us. He dropped to his knees, pounding the concrete with both fists until his skin split open. Again. Again.

"WHY?! WHY THEM?!"

None of us moved.

His sobs were violent. Deep and raw.

"I did everything right! I stayed hopeful! I kept moving!" he shouted to the void. "And they still died like animals! What's the damn point?!"

His voice cracked, rage spilling into grief and back again. "Is this what you people do?! March through death like it's another fucking Tuesday?!"

Charles looked down, jaw clenched so hard his teeth clicked.

Bryan stood slowly, staring us down. "Why are you even out here, huh? Playing hero? You military types always have a reason."

CJ opened his mouth, but Charles stepped forward.

"We're here to get the President to an extraction point. That's it."

Bryan blinked, then looked to me. "Is that true?"

I nodded. "There's a cure. We're trying to save what's left of the world."

Bryan scoffed. "Of course. The world. Gotta save the world. And what about the people already gone? Huh? My girls—my wife—your mission going to bring them back?"

Silence.

"No," Charles said finally. "But stopping now makes their deaths worthless."

Bryan stepped in close, fury burning behind his eyes. "Don't you dare talk about worth. You think a speech is going to fix this?"

"I didn't say that," Charles growled. "But wallowing in it doesn't fix it either."

Bryan shoved him. "Wallowing? You think this is wallowing? I just held my daughter's arm in my goddamn hand!"

Charles didn't budge. "You think you're the only one who lost someone?"

"Feels like it," Bryan spat.

"You didn't know Sheila," Charles said, voice suddenly quieter—more strained.

Bryan furrowed his brow. "The woman who died?"

Charles took a slow step forward. "She was more than that. She… she *was* this team. She got us through every street, every alley, every kill zone. She never froze. Never panicked. Always knew the next move."

Bryan blinked. "And now she's gone?"

Charles nodded once. His voice cracked. "Yeah. She's gone."

Bryan looked around at all of us—at our hollow eyes, at Shaun's trembling hands, at CJ's slumped shoulders.

"I didn't know," he said, his voice soft for the first time. "I didn't know she meant that much."

"She was my wife," Charles said through gritted teeth. "And I couldn't save her."

Silence.

"I didn't know," Bryan repeated, taking a step back.

Something shifted in him. The guilt bled into rage again—self-inflicted now. "I didn't know... and here I am bitching at you."

Charles shook his head slowly. "We all break. You're not the first. You won't be the last."

Then suddenly Bryan exploded again, punching the wall so hard that a chunk of plaster broke off.

"FUCK THIS WORLD!" he screamed. "FUCK THIS—EVERYTHING!"

He turned and swung at a nearby trash bin, sending it crashing into a wall.

"I SHOULD'VE DIED IN THAT HOUSE WITH THEM!"

"No," I said firmly. "You shouldn't have."

Bryan looked at me, tears streaking down his face.

"You're still here," I said. "That means something."

He laughed bitterly, eyes unfocused. "Yeah? You're gonna tell me it's fate? Destiny?"

"No," I said. "But maybe it's a chance. A second chance."

Bryan didn't respond. His breathing was ragged, his shoulders still heaving.

Charles walked over, reached into his jacket, and silently handed Bryan one of his knives.

Bryan stared at it, then took it with shaking hands.

"No more running," Charles said.

Bryan nodded once. "Yeah. No more running."

And for now, that was enough.

TEN MILES

The world felt wrong.

The infected weren't coming in waves anymore. No screeching hordes, no frantic swarms. Just silence, broken by the soft crunch of broken glass under our boots and the occasional groan of a lone straggler stumbling from the shadows.

Shaun swept his rifle across an empty alley, then lowered it. "Where the hell is everyone?"

CJ scanned the rooftops, his voice uneasy. "Too damn quiet. I don't trust it."

But Bryan didn't speak. He moved ahead of the group, a storm barely held together. He wasn't looking for safety — he was hunting. Every infected that shambled too close was met with raw, merciless force. A thick combat knife in one hand, a blood-slick crowbar in the other. Every swing came with fury. Every kill came with grief.

One infected reached out with broken fingers, moaning. Bryan didn't flinch. He shoved the crowbar up under its chin, twisting until bone cracked. The thing collapsed at his feet. Bryan stood over it, chest heaving, eyes red.

None of us said a word. What could we say?

"Ten miles out," Charles muttered finally, checking the worn, blood-specked map. "Almost there."

Almost.

We were walking through hell, but the devil wasn't chasing us anymore. That's what scared me the most.

Bryan wiped blood from his face with the sleeve of his shirt, staring down at another corpse like he expected it to apologize. He didn't cry. He didn't speak. But the way he fought — it screamed.

We kept moving, slow and tense, shadows stretching longer than they should have. Each step toward the extraction point felt heavier, like it might be our last.

The silence wasn't peace. It was a warning.

The road narrowed into a ruined residential stretch — houses sagging under their own weight, mailboxes rusted shut, cars long since looted and burned. The sky above was a dull slate gray, clouds threatening a storm that never quite came. Everything smelled like wet ash and old blood.

Bryan walked ahead of us still, silent, coated in dried gore. His grip on the crowbar hadn't loosened in miles. I watched him smash the skull of a crawling infected without even breaking stride.

CJ finally muttered, "He's gonna tear himself apart."

"No," Shaun said, quieter. "He already has."

We didn't interrupt him. Whatever storm raged inside Bryan needed space, and none of us had the right to pull him out of it just yet. Grief did that to a man — turned you into a hammer with nothing left to build.

Charles slowed near a fence, squatting behind it and motioning the rest of us forward. "Eyes open," he ordered. "Still too quiet. I don't like it."

We fanned out, sweeping the nearby houses for any sign of movement. Inside one, we found a half-eaten dog, ribs showing. In another, just bloodstains and an old teddy bear in a corner.

CJ crouched beside a corpse in the street, checking its clothing. "Looks recent," he whispered. "Whoever did this… they're not far."

Shaun kicked open the door of a nearby shed, then relaxed when it revealed only a toppled lawnmower and some rusted tools. "No signs of feeding frenzy," he said. "It's like they left."

"Or were called away," Charles muttered. "Mob behavior. Just like Mom— just like Sheila figured."

Bryan stiffened, just a flicker. Then he kept walking, down the middle of the cracked street like a ghost. I saw his jaw tighten. No words came.

We followed. Ten miles from salvation, and somehow it felt further than ever.

We heard them before we saw them — the deep, rhythmic thuds of hundreds of feet trampling cracked asphalt in sync. The kind of sound you feel in your ribs.

Charles raised his fist, and the team dropped low behind an abandoned box truck. I crouched last, my breathing already quickening. We peered through a smashed window.

There they were.

A herd — but not like the others.

These weren't aimless biters stumbling into cars and tripping over each other. They moved in formation. Spread across the street but tight enough to protect each other. Heads low, eyes scanning. They moved around obstacles instead of over them. One of them, limping with a twisted leg, stopped at a fallen comrade and picked up a jagged metal rod, dragging it behind him.

Shaun whispered, "What the hell…"

CJ's voice was quiet but urgent. "They're hunting. Like a pack."

Bryan gritted his teeth. His fingers flexed around the crowbar. "Let me at 'em."

"No," Charles snapped. "They're not rushing us. That means they don't know we're here. Yet."

We watched in tense silence as the herd reached an overturned city bus… and split. Half veered around the left side of the street, while the other half flanked right — like they were clearing the path ahead.

I leaned closer to CJ. "That's not instinct. That's coordination."

"Yeah," CJ said. "They're getting smarter."

Shaun didn't blink. "Or someone's leading them."

For a moment, none of us moved. I could hear my pulse in my ears.

Then, one of the infected stopped. Its head snapped toward the truck. Not slow. Not curious. Sharp. Intentional.

Charles hissed, "We're burned."

The creature let out a low, guttural growl — and suddenly the others turned.

"MOVE!" Charles shouted.

We bolted from cover as the herd screamed and charged. Bryan met the first one mid-sprint, swinging his crowbar like an axe and splitting its head with a savage roar. Shaun and CJ flanked him, blades out, slashing anything that got too close. I fired my pistol once — missed — then just ran.

The group pulled back into an alleyway, fighting in tight quarters. Shaun kicked one into a dumpster. CJ slit another's throat, blood spraying across his face. Bryan smashed skulls like they were glass.

They came at us with a purpose. With patience. Like they knew who we were.

It was CJ who realized it first. "They're trying to pin us in! They're herding us like cattle!"

"NOT TODAY!" Charles shouted, launching a kick that sent one crashing into a brick wall.

We tore through them in a savage burst of steel and bone. It was brutal, bloody, and desperate. And when the last one dropped, panting, all of us stood covered in gore, surrounded by twitching bodies.

The silence that followed was deeper than before.

Shaun, shaking slightly, muttered, "We're running out of time."

Charles wiped blood from his face, jaw clenched. "We keep moving. And we don't stop."

And we didn't.

The alley spat us back out into a mangled intersection, flanked by broken storefronts and flipped-over sedans. Blood coated the walls. Shattered glass crunched beneath our boots. We didn't speak. We just moved.

That's when we heard it — not a scream, not a snarl.

A *clicking* noise. Repetitive. Calculated. Almost mechanical.

Shaun stopped in his tracks. "You hear that?"

"Yeah," I whispered. "Too clean to be a walker."

The noise echoed again, closer this time. And then… it appeared.

Tall. Pale. Mutated beyond anything we'd seen. Its torso stretched unnaturally, ribs bowed outward, exposing muscles that pulsed with each breath. Its arms were long — far too long — knuckles dragging the pavement like a gorilla. But its eyes… its eyes were what stopped us cold.

They were focused. Calculating.

It didn't roar.

It charged.

"MOVE!" Charles shouted.

The ground trembled as it sprinted at us on all fours like a demon let loose. Bryan was the first to react, throwing his body into a tackle that knocked one of the smaller infected into its path — a delay that bought us maybe two seconds.

Then it hit.

A car exploded beside us as the creature hurled a full-bodied infected like a wrecking ball. The shockwave shattered our formation.

"Shaun! Mr. President!" Charles yelled.

But it was too late. A collapsing fire escape slammed between us and the others.

Dust clouded the street. I stumbled, hand in Shaun's grip as he pulled me behind cover. We were cut off.

"Shaun?" CJ's voice crackled over the comms, static and panic. "Shaun! Can you hear me?"

"We're good!" Shaun shouted back, shielding me from the debris. "What's your status?!"

"Separated," Charles barked. "CJ's with me. We're circling north!"

"Where's Bryan?" I asked.

There was no answer.

Shaun spun around, looking through the broken windows, through the chaos. "He's not with either group."

The silence was heavy.

Then came a distant roar. Not the herd. Not the smarter infected. It was Bryan.

Alone.

Raging.

We had no line of sight, no backup, no way to regroup fast.

Shaun's jaw tensed. He looked at me. "We move. Quiet. Fast. Stay low. And don't stop unless I tell you."

I nodded, still shaken.

As we moved, I caught one last glimpse of the mutant climbing over a half-destroyed pharmacy wall. It wasn't chasing anymore. It was watching.

Hunting.

Not like prey.

Like a rival.

STEEL AND SHADOW

The street was silent.

Too silent.

I could still hear the chaos behind us — metal crashing, groans echoing, the others shouting into comms — but here, it was just me and Shaun.

And the horde.

Fifty of them.

Mindless, starving, bone-thin, and fast.

They came around the corner like a tidal wave of rot and hunger, screaming without voices, jaws hanging open, arms flailing like broken machines. No strategy. Just overwhelming numbers.

Shaun stood between me and them.

No rifle. No mags left. Just a combat knife in one hand, a utility blade in the other — one serrated, one clean. Blood already covered his arms. His breath was steady. His eyes locked.

He didn't flinch.

Didn't look back.

"Stay behind me," he muttered, low and cold. "No matter what."

I froze. "Shaun—"

"I got this," he said. Then stepped forward.

And hell met steel.

The first infected lunged, teeth bared — Shaun ducked low and drove his serrated blade into its neck, spun, and used its own momentum to sling it into the next. He was already moving before it hit the ground.

He moved like smoke. Controlled. Efficient. A whirlwind of slashes and stabs, every motion deliberate. One blade cut, the other blocked. Knees, throats, eyes — he didn't waste a single strike.

A runner got close enough to graze my jacket.

Before I could react, Shaun *appeared*, grabbed its jaw, and slammed the knife upward through its mouth, spine cracking on the way down. Blood sprayed across his face, but his expression didn't change.

Ten down. Then twenty. Then more.

He didn't stop.

A crawler latched onto his ankle — he stomped its skull without breaking stride.

Another tried to blindside him from a parked car — he ducked under the swing, slit its Achilles, and gutted it in one fluid movement.

The pavement became a canvas of red.

My ears rang from the silence in his fight. No war cries. No wasted words.

Just breath. Focus. Resolve.

By the time the last one collapsed in front of him, twitching and headless, Shaun stood over the bodies like a monument carved from war.

Steam rose from his skin in the cold air. Blood dripped off both blades.

He turned to me, chest rising slowly.

"Still breathing?" he asked, like he'd just finished a workout.

I nodded, stunned. "You… that was fifty."

"Fifty sloppy ones," he said. "I'll worry when they send sixty."

And then he walked past me like it was nothing.

But I saw the truth in his eyes as he passed:

It wasn't nothing.

It was *everything*.

The city had a way of holding its breath after violence.

Broken windows whispered in the wind. Blood pooled in gutters. The stink of death lingered on everything — skin, clothes, breath — but somehow, silence wrapped around us again.

Shaun moved ahead of me, blades still wet but now sheathed. His stride was smooth, focused. Not tense. Just… prepared. Like he was always waiting for the next fight, and nothing would catch him off guard again.

My heartbeat still hadn't slowed from the last encounter. He'd just cut down fifty infected. I'd never seen anything like it — not in any military training, not in any film, not in any nightmare.

He was calm now. Too calm.

We ducked through the crumbling shell of a storefront, glass crunching beneath our boots.

Then static crackled in Shaun's comm.

"Shaun. Hector. This is Viper Two."

Shaun froze and tapped his earpiece. "Copy."

"We've cleared a path and are circling southeast. There's a rendezvous ahead. Look for the courthouse on 3rd. Basement's secure."

"Copy that," Shaun said. "ETA… maybe forty minutes."

"Keep him safe."

"Always."

The channel went silent.

We kept moving.

It was another minute before I spoke. "You don't talk much."

"Not when I'm working," Shaun said.

I nodded. "You're always working."

He glanced back at me — not annoyed. Just… tired.

"It's how I keep from thinking."

We passed a rusted-out ambulance, doors still swinging in the wind. A broken IV bag dangled from the roof like a ghost of the world before.

"You were close with her," I said.

Shaun didn't answer right away. He just kept walking.

Then finally: "Yeah. Mom knew how to shut us all up. Even Dad."

"That's a skill," I said.

Shaun smirked. "More like a superpower."

We walked in silence again. No infected. Just the wind and our footsteps.

I looked over at him — not as a soldier, not even as a protector.

Just a son carrying a wound no one could see.

"You're the reason I'm still breathing," I said. "Back there… that wasn't luck."

Shaun shrugged. "No. That was rage."

He looked ahead.

"And I'm not done using it."

The air changed.

One block from the courthouse, the wind shifted — from stale and sour to *wrong*. It smelled like heat. Like blood that hadn't cooled yet. My skin prickled.

Shaun stopped moving.

I almost bumped into him. "What is it?"

He didn't answer. Just crouched, knife already drawn, eyes scanning the shadows ahead.

A guttural *click* echoed from somewhere behind the cars.

Then a second one answered… from above.

Shaun's eyes narrowed.

"Back up," he said. "Quietly."

I obeyed.

And then it dropped.

The mutated thing came down from a fire escape like a nightmare — six feet tall but hunched low, with arms too long and muscles twitching like live wires. Its face was a mess of scars, jaw split down the middle like someone had taken an axe to it. Its eyes? Focused.

And it didn't charge.

It *studied* us.

"This one's smart," Shaun muttered, sliding between me and it. "Back into the alley. If it flanks, we're screwed."

We moved, slow and quiet — but not quiet enough.

It leapt, landing behind us, cutting off our exit.

"Shit," I breathed.

Shaun didn't hesitate. "It's not attacking yet. It's watching."

He scanned the alley — dumpsters, shattered brick walls, metal piping, broken glass.

Then his eyes landed on an exposed gas line running along the wall.

I saw the plan form in his head *before* he moved.

"Stay behind the crate," he said. "When I say duck — *duck.*"

"Shaun—"

"Do it."

The thing hissed and stepped forward.

Shaun flicked his knife into a reverse grip, kicked a trash can into the creature's path — not to hurt it, but to redirect it. It lunged, swiping wild.

Shaun slid under its swing, slashed across its calf, rolled behind the creature, and cut the gas line with one clean motion.

It hissed open. The alley was filled with the sharp scent of gas.

He moved fast — grabbed a flare from his belt, lit it, and threw it past the creature, toward the leaking pipe.

"Duck!"

I dove behind the crate.

The flare hit the gas line. The explosion roared down the alley like a dragon's breath — not enough to level the block, but more than enough to engulf the creature in flames.

It shrieked, flailing, flesh boiling.

Shaun didn't wait. He charged through the smoke, drove his blade up under its chin, twisted hard, and shoved it into the wall as the fire died around them.

The thing dropped.

Dead.

He turned, coated in ash and blood, and walked over like it was routine.

"You good?" he asked.

"I… yeah," I stammered, sitting up from behind the crate.

"Smart bastard," he said, nodding at the body. "But not smart enough."

I stood, still stunned. "You planned all that in ten seconds."

Shaun wiped his knife on his pant leg and sheathed it.

"Ten seconds is generous."

And with that, he kept walking — calm, controlled.

Like it was just another chess piece removed from the board.

The echo of the explosion hadn't faded when the growls came.

Then the pounding.

Then the stampede.

Dozens of infected, snarling and sprinting, poured into the street like a dam had burst. Shattered bodies twisted through broken glass and flame. They weren't confused. They weren't frantic.

They were *focused*.

Shaun stepped in front of me, blades out, blood already drying on his sleeves. He didn't speak. Just stared into the oncoming wave like he'd seen it all before — and wasn't impressed.

But I saw the fatigue.

His body was slowing, his movements tighter. That last fight had drained him, and we both knew it.

The first infected lunged — Shaun sidestepped and buried his knife in its eye. Another followed. He spun, slashed its throat, and used its momentum to shove it into a third. He fought with practiced brutality, but his shoulders were heavier. His breathing is louder.

I watched him fight off ten. Then twelve. Then fifteen.

But for every one that fell, three more surged forward.

One caught him with a wild swing — raked its claws across his shoulder. The blade didn't cut deep, but it staggered him. Another charged — he dropped low and slammed it into the ground.

His arm trembled when he tried to stand.

"Shaun!" I started forward.

He raised one hand. "I said, *stay back!*"

Then the mutated infected came down like thunder.

It landed hard, crushing the body of a dead walker beneath its clawed feet. Seven feet tall. Shoulders like armor plating. A face like melted bone. It didn't snarl. It just looked at Shaun.

Then charged.

Shaun roared, meeting it head-on with both blades. He got in two good slashes — one across the knee, another across the side — before the thing slammed him backward into a parked car. The metal screamed as Shaun hit it full-force, falling to his knees.

He coughed hard, spit in the dirt, and tried to rise.

The mutated raised a jagged arm, claws ready to tear through him.

Then—

BANG.

A shot cracked through the alley.

BANG. BANG. BANG.

The mutated's skull snapped back with each hit — until the fourth round drilled through its jaw and dropped it like a bag of wet meat beside Shaun.

Smoke still curled off the barrel of the rifle.

And there — stumbling through flame and shadow — was Bryan.

Blood streaked across his brow. His jacket was torn. He clutched his ribs, limping. But his grip on the rifle was firm, eyes burning with fire.

He stepped closer, chest heaving, and grinned just enough to show teeth.

"Stack 5... at your service."

Shaun looked up, groaning, breath shallow but steady.

"Took your damn time," he muttered.

Bryan lowered his rifle and dropped to one knee beside him. "Gotta make an entrance."

I stepped in, helping Shaun sit up, checking him over.

No bites. No deep wounds. Just bruises, blood, and exhaustion.

Same with Bryan.

They were beaten. Battered.

But they were alive.

And for now, *that* was enough.

The street was still for a moment.

Shaun leaned against the crumpled van, bleeding from scrapes, breathing hard but alive. Bryan knelt beside him, equally wrecked, body shaking from exhaustion.

"Here," Bryan said, reaching into his jacket and pulling out a small, taped bundle — a magazine with only a few bullets left. "Found it in a broken-down squad car back on 6th. Figured you'd need it more than me."

Shaun stared at it, then at him.

"You're giving me your last rounds?" he asked, voice rasping.

Bryan gave a tired grin. "Man, look at me. I barely got enough blood to finish a jog, let alone another fight. You're the one who doesn't miss."

Shaun hesitated, then took the mag and loaded it into his rifle with a *click*.

"Stack 5," he muttered. "Still full of bad ideas."

"Only the best ones," Bryan smirked.

I moved to help lift Shaun, but that moment of peace was shattered with the scream of another group of infected — faster, angrier, bounding over parked cars and debris like they were chasing blood because they were.

Bryan was the first to react.

He pushed Shaun and me toward the cover of a delivery truck, then stepped into the open, standing between us and the horde.

"NO!" I shouted. "You're hurt—"

"Yeah, and I'm still prettier than them," he muttered.

And then he opened fire.

Every shot was perfect. Controlled bursts. Kneecaps, skulls, throats. The kind of fire you laid down when there was no plan except to *buy time*.

"GO!" he shouted. "MOVE!"

We did.

Until one of the infected — a half-mutated one with a twisted spine and bone spikes jutting from its ribs — broke from the pack and *charged* Shaun.

Bryan turned without thinking.

He threw himself into its path, slamming into it shoulder-first, dragging it into the wall. They struggled, fists and claws, blood flying across the alley.

Then it happened.

The thing drove a broken rebar through Bryan's side.

The sound it made — not a scream, not a gasp. Just a sharp *exhale,* like he'd been punched in the soul.

"BRYAN!" Shaun roared, spinning and unloading the rest of the clip into the thing's head. It dropped — finally dead.

Bryan slumped to one knee, hand pressing into the hole in his side. Blood poured fast.

But he didn't fall.

He *gritted his teeth and stayed up.*

Just as the street behind us lit up with a flashlight beam and two figures charged forward—

"SHAUN!"

"HECTOR!"

Charles and CJ.

They were sprinting, Blades out, eyes wide.

Shaun limped to Bryan and caught him just before he collapsed fully. Bryan was shaking, blood running through his fingers.

CJ dropped beside him, pulling gauze from his kit. "Jesus, that's a hole."

Bryan tried to smile. "Yeah, well... Stack 5 doesn't go out *quietly.*"

Charles knelt on the other side, hand on Bryan's shoulder, jaw clenched. "We got you. You hear me? We got you."

Bryan coughed — and it was wet — but nodded once. "Told you I wasn't done…"

He didn't pass out.

He *refused* to.

We wrapped him tight. Lifted him slow. Carried him like the hero he'd just proved himself to be — again.

And as the chapter closed around us, blood on the street, the moon above cracked in smoke and ash—

We were together.

For now.

And still breathing.

10

FATHER AND SON

—Earlier—

The blast split us like a blade.

Steel, concrete, and fire poured between our team. The last thing I saw was CJ getting yanked backward by Charles as a fire escape came crashing down, sealing them off from us.

Shaun's voice crackled in my ear:
"We're good! Hector's with me! What's your status?!"

"Separated," Charles snapped. His voice was tight. Focused. "CJ's with me. We'll circle north and head for the courthouse. Stick to the plan."

There was a pause.

Then my voice over the comm:

"…Where's Bryan?"

No answer.

And then the channel went dead.

Charles and CJ moved fast — not quiet, not subtle, just fast. The chaos had already drawn the attention of the infected, and they weren't about to get pinned in the open.

No ammo. Just knives, fists, and fury.

They cut down two infected in the alley behind the blast zone — quick, surgical work. Charles took one to the ground and ended it with his boot. CJ slashed the other's hamstring and buried his knife under its jaw. The movements weren't pretty — they were exhausted, deliberate, and exact.

CJ wiped his blade on his pants. "We're blind. Radios are trash past fifty feet. We've gotta trust they're headed the same direction."

Charles was already moving. "They are. Shaun knows where the rendezvous is. And Hector's not getting left behind, but I will make sure I tell him on the radio."

Shaun. Hector. This is Viper Two."

"We've cleared a path and are circling southeast. There's a rendezvous ahead. Look for the courthouse on 3rd. Basement's secure."

"Copy." Shaun's voice is coming over on the comms.

They then climbed over a half-collapsed chain-link fence and dropped into a narrow service alley, sidestepping a burned-out patrol car and ducking through the remnants of an old loading dock. Everything reeked — smoke, rot, engine oil.

CJ paused.

Blood. Not pooled — smeared. A drag mark near a broken window.

He crouched beside it. "This was recent. Someone hurt bad… but not bleeding out."

Charles knelt, ran two fingers across the dried edge. "Boot print. Heavy. Deep heel. Bryan."

CJ raised an eyebrow. "You sure?"

"Man's built like a tank," Charles muttered. "Leaves a trail like one too."

They kept moving, now aware they weren't forging a new path — they were following one. Through an old tailor shop, they found broken glass scattered across the floor and the unmistakable scuff marks of a fight. A few lone infected were already down, crumpled with crushed skulls or severed throats.

CJ nudged one with his boot. "Bryan again?"

Charles didn't answer. He just kept walking.

They crossed a main road next — ducked under a fallen streetlight, cut through the burned skeleton of a post office, and emerged onto 3rd Street.

Then CJ froze.

A dumpster had been shoved to the side. A perfect barricade. Quick, desperate — but tactical.

CJ's voice dropped. "That's Bryan."

Charles looked around the intersection — the courthouse tower just barely visible in the haze ahead.

They weren't just tracking the others anymore.

They were following their family's path.

Step by step.

Bleeding ground for bleeding ground.

They didn't hear the horde coming.

They felt it.

A vibration in the ground. Subtle at first — like distant thunder under their boots.

Charles turned his head slightly. "You feel that?"

CJ's knife was already back in his hand. "Yeah. Something big."

Then the sound came — a wall of snarls, screeches, and stomping footsteps. In seconds, the alley ahead exploded with movement as the infected poured out from broken buildings, tunnels, and even storm drains. Dozens. More.

No escape route.

No fire support.

And no ammo.

Charles glanced at CJ. "Ready?"

CJ gave a crooked grin. "Born for it."

And then they charged.

Father and son — no time for talk, just instinct. Years of missions, drills, dinners, and silent understanding all igniting in one synchronized assault.

Charles moved like a freight train. Knife in one hand, a busted metal pipe in the other. He crashed into the horde first, slamming a runner back into a car with his shoulder, then dragging the pipe across its skull with a crunch.

CJ danced around him — agile, brutal. One infected lunged toward Charles' blind side — CJ stepped in, dropped it with a hamstring slice and throat jab, then spun to intercept a second one crawling from under a vehicle.

They moved like they'd rehearsed this chaos.

"Six on your right!" CJ shouted.

"I've got four!" Charles roared.

"Math's off."

Charles elbowed a biter in the face, sending teeth skittering across the pavement. "Shut up and swing."

CJ kicked one back into the wall and stabbed low, just above the pelvis, then again through the eye socket. "Still think you're faster than me, old man?"

"You wanna compare kill counts, let's live through this first."

The horde pressed harder. Bodies piled. Screams filled the alley. Claws raked skin. One of the infected grabbed CJ's arm — Charles snapped its wrist with a pipe strike, then planted his blade in its temple.

"Thanks, Dad."

"You're welcome."

They were losing ground — but not spirit. Blood slicked their sleeves. Arms ached. Breaths came harder. Still, they didn't stop. Couldn't stop.

One thing became clear to anyone watching: this wasn't just survival.

It was vengeance.

For Sheila.

For the hell they'd walked through just to see their mother/wife alive one more time.

Then — like a curse being lifted — the final infected dropped. Its head hit the concrete with a wet slap, blood soaking the cracks beneath it.

Charles dropped to one knee, panting hard. CJ leaned against the wall, knife still trembling in his grip.

"Fuck," CJ muttered.

Charles wiped sweat from his eyes with a bloody forearm. "We need to find them. Now."

They looked up — the courthouse was just two blocks away.

Still bleeding ground.

But they were closing in.

They were one block out when the explosion hit.

A thunderclap of fire and debris shook the street ahead — the kind of sound that made your heart skip before your brain even caught up. Flame burst into the sky beyond the rooftops, black smoke rising like a signal flare from hell.

Charles and CJ both froze mid-stride.

"Shaun," Charles breathed. "That's him."

CJ didn't argue. He was already sprinting.

They cut through a narrow passage between two collapsed apartment buildings, boots slamming against the cracked pavement, dodging toppled debris, broken pipes, and infected carcasses.

As they turned the final corner—

They saw it.

A flood of infected pouring from every direction, drawn like flies to the fire. It wasn't a horde — it was a feeding frenzy, all racing toward where the explosion had come from. Toward Shaun. Toward Hector.

CJ grabbed Charles by the shoulder, pulling him into cover behind a derelict city bus as a cluster of infected tore past. Too many to fight. Too many to chase.

And then—

They saw him.

Just beyond the edge of the horde, maybe forty yards up, sprinting like a man possessed—

Bryan.

"Holy shit…" CJ whispered.

He wasn't limping anymore. He wasn't tired. He wasn't human. He was a storm.

His axe tore through two infected with a single swing, carving bodies down like grass. Blood sprayed, limbs flew. One infected latched onto his back — he slammed it into a wall without breaking stride. Another reached for his leg — he stomped its skull mid-run and kept going.

His face was streaked with blood — some his, most not. His coat was shredded, skin exposed beneath, muscles straining with every step. And he was headed straight for the explosion.

"Stack 5," Charles muttered, voice tight with something like awe. "He's not running away…"

CJ exhaled. "He's running into it."

The building where the smoke still rolled out — they knew it now. The old federal annex, connected to the courthouse's side entrance.

Where Shaun was.

Where Hector was.

Charles looked at CJ. "We move now. No detours. No breaks. You see a biter, drop it. Don't play with your food."

CJ flipped his knife in his hand. "Right behind you."

They charged into the fire Bryan had lit.

They were closing in fast now — too fast.

Charles and CJ turned down the final block, eyes burning from smoke and fire. The air was thick with the scent of rot and gunpowder, but it wasn't the smell that told them they were close.

It was Shaun's voice.

"I SAID STAY BACK!"

Charles didn't hesitate. He vaulted a shattered railing and landed hard on the broken sidewalk below. CJ dropped beside him, knives out, already moving.

In front of them, the horde was still thick — a flowing mass of rotting flesh and snarling mouths all converging on the chaos. But their formation was loose. Scattered.

This was the bottleneck.
The one Stack 5 had torn open.

"Cut through!" Charles barked. "We punch a hole now, or they don't make it!"

CJ didn't answer — he was already slicing.

One infected lunged from behind a rusted car — Charles intercepted it mid-stride, grabbed its collar, and slammed it into the pavement. A sickening crunch echoed, followed by silence.

CJ was faster — precise. He ducked under a reaching claw, slashed across a biter's eyes, then spun and stabbed another in the chest so hard the blade punched out its back.

They were a blur — a two-man storm tearing into the rear flank of the horde.

"WE'RE CLEARING THEM!" CJ shouted between heavy breaths.

"KEEP PUSHING!" Charles bellowed.

Then came the gunfire.

One shot — BANG.
Then three more.

And then the voice:

"STACK 5 AT YOUR SERVICE!"

It rang out like a war cry, booming over the blood and screams.

Charles froze for half a second, eyes widening.

"That's Bryan."

CJ nodded, almost grinning. "He made it."

They couldn't see him — but they could feel the ripple through the horde. Bodies falling. Heads bursting. Momentum shifting.

Then came my voice, strained and desperate through the comms:

"NO! You're hurt!"

More gunshots cracked through the street.

Then Bryan's voice boomed through the chaos:

"GO! MOVE!"

A crash — something heavy slamming into a wall.

Then Shaun:

"BRYAN!"

Charles and CJ cut down the last infected in their path with feral speed. One biter leapt from a second-story balcony, landing inches from Charles — he drove his blade through its throat and didn't even break stride.

CJ dropped the last runner with a brutal elbow and a boot to the jaw.

Then the street opened up — the courthouse's side wall finally in sight.

Fires flickered at the base.

Smoke rolled across the concrete like a curtain.

The fight was still going.

But the family was almost whole.

The flames were still licking the base of the courthouse when they broke through the last of the infected.

"SHAUN!"
"HECTOR!"

Charles and CJ.

They were sprinting, blades out, eyes wide — searching through smoke, firelight flickering across their bloodstained gear.

I turned, breath caught in my throat, just as Shaun dropped to one knee beside Bryan. He barely caught him before Bryan collapsed fully. Bryan was trembling, his blood pooling fast through the hole in his side, staining Shaun's hands.

CJ hit the ground beside them, already tearing through his medkit.

"Jesus," he muttered, pressing gauze to the wound. "That's a hole."

Bryan let out a rough breath that was almost a laugh. "Yeah, well… Stack 5 doesn't go out quietly."

Charles knelt on the other side, one hand on Bryan's shoulder, jaw locked like it was the only thing keeping him from shattering.

"We got you," he said, voice steady but low. "You hear me? We got you."

Bryan coughed — wet, but controlled. His skin was pale, his eyes glassy, but he still nodded.

"Told you I wasn't done…"

He didn't pass out.

He refused to.

We worked fast — CJ doing most of it, hands stained with blood and ash. Charles kept pressure, Shaun kept guard. I stood over them all, watching the doorway, trying to breathe.

No more infected came.

Not yet.

We wrapped Bryan tight. Lifted him slow.

Carried him like the hero he'd just proven himself to be —
again.

He never complained. Never whimpered. He grit his teeth and leaned on us, blood dripping behind him, one hand still clenched in a fist, like he had more fight left if anyone dared come for us again.

The moon hung above us, blurred through the smoke. Broken. Distant.

But we were here.

Together.

Wounded. Shaken. Alive.

And for the first time in what felt like days, I felt something close to hope.

For now...

We were still breathing.

11

ASHSTEP

The courthouse was quiet now.

No more screams. No more gunfire. Just the low, steady crackle of small fires outside and the shallow breathing of a dying man.

Bryan lay on a stone bench beneath the remnants of a stained-glass skylight. The light that filtered through was weak and dusty — like even the sun wasn't sure it wanted to see what came next.

CJ knelt beside him, hands soaked red, doing everything he could with what little he had left. The gauze was used up. The pressure dressings had turned dark and heavy. His voice was soft now, less urgent — more like pleading.

Shaun sat beside Bryan. Not guarding. Not pacing. Just... sitting.

Exhaustion dripped from his posture like sweat. He looked like someone who had nothing left to fight with. But he stayed beside Bryan, shoulder to shoulder, as if that meant something more than medicine ever could.

I crouched on the other side, close enough to hear Bryan's breath hitch. His chest rose unevenly. Eyes half-lidded. But he was still there.

"Hey," I said gently.

His eyes twitched open. "Yo, Prez…"

He tried to smile, but it came out broken. "I make it?"

"Yeah," I said, swallowing hard. "You made it."

"Damn right I did."

A beat passed. Then he glanced at Shaun.

"You alright?"

Shaun didn't speak. Just gave a slow nod.

"Good…" Bryan whispered. "Didn't want my last act to be a f***ing *oops.*"

CJ chuckled through clenched teeth. "It was *close*, man."

Bryan shifted, winced, and let out a weak laugh. "You always were a critic."

He looked back at me. "You asked me… back when we first met… about my dream. The store."

I nodded. "Still want to hear it."

Shaun leaned in, watching him.

Bryan's voice cracked. "I didn't want to make shoes to sell. I wanted to make something for people like us. People who walk through hell and keep walking. I told my girls it wasn't about looking cool. It was about making it to the next day."

He paused, eyes fluttering shut, but then forced them open.

"I had a name. Stupid maybe… but real."

We leaned in.

He smiled softly.

"Ashstep."

CJ whispered it back. "Ashstep?"

"Yeah…" Bryan said, voice barely there. "Walk through fire, leave a mark…"

His next breath rattled in his chest.

"I just wanted to build something… that lasted. Something they could wear and remember me by. My girls… they'd run around the kitchen yelling the name. 'Dad's gonna be famous!' they said. Said it like it was already true."

His hand twitched.

"They'd say… one day… they'd wear a pair of Ashsteps to school and tell everyone—"

And then…

He stopped.

Mid-sentence. Mid-breath.

No gasp.

No scream.

Just silence.

CJ froze. His hand was still on the bandage. His lip is trembling.

Shaun turned away, fists clenched. He didn't say a word. Didn't need to.

Charles stood by the doorway. Still. Silent. He didn't look back, but one hand slowly reached up to the back of his neck — like he'd felt something leave.

I reached forward and closed Bryan's eyes, my vision swimming.

He didn't get to finish his sentence.

But he'd said enough.

We lost Stack 5.

And yet somehow... the fire he walked through still warmed us.

Ashstep.

We didn't move for a long time.

Bryan lay still beneath a tattered sheet CJ had torn from a courthouse banner. His axe rested beside him. His blood had stopped pooling, but it hadn't stopped staining.

The only sounds were boots shifting and breath. No one spoke. Not even Shaun.

CJ leaned against a cracked pillar, the city map crushed in his grip. Charles stood with his arms crossed, face unreadable, but his eyes… they didn't blink. Shaun sat alone, elbows on his knees, staring at the bench where Bryan had died — his hands still red.

I stood.

Not because I wanted to. Because I *had* to.

"We lost one of the best men I've ever met," I said, my voice low. "And we didn't lose him because he was weak. Or careless. We lost him because he gave every piece of himself so we wouldn't have to."

CJ looked down. Charles clenched his jaw.

"Bryan didn't die on some podium," I continued. "He didn't get a folded flag or final salute. He died in a broken courthouse, covered in blood, with a dream he never got to finish — a dream of building something better than this."

Shaun shifted slightly.

I looked at them each in turn.

"That dream… that *stupid, beautiful dream…* is the reason we keep going. Because if we stop now, if we let this place eat us, then everything Bryan fought for… everything we've *all* lost… dies with us."

I stepped closer to the bench.

"He deserved more. So we give it to him the only way we can."

I pointed to the map in CJ's hands. "We finish the mission."

CJ crouched slowly, unrolling the map across a flat slab of marble.

"We're here," he said, tapping the edge of the courthouse. "Extraction's 8 miles southeast. One stretch of open road, a couple of alley loops. There's a tunnel under District 14 — if we can clear it, we avoid two hot zones completely."

Charles finally moved beside him. "What's between us and the tunnel?"

CJ didn't hesitate. "One residential choke point. Overrun three weeks ago. Could be empty now. Could be worse."

"Resources?" I asked.

CJ checked his inventory.

"One and a half canteens. No meds. No ammo. Just steel and stubbornness."

"Then we move on to steel and stubbornness," Charles muttered.

Shaun finally stood.

Not fast. Not dramatically. Just… solid. Focused.

"Let's get going before the wrong kind of silence finds us."

CJ folded the map and looked at me. "You lead, sir."

I glanced back at Bryan one last time.

We'd bury him with our silence.

We'd honor him with our fire.

And we'd finish the job he died to protect.

We left the courthouse in silence.

No one said a word.

CJ took point, the map folded and tucked into the strap across his chest. Shaun walked beside me, knife drawn, eyes always forward. Charles covered our rear, blade in hand, like it was part of him.

Bryan's body stayed behind.

There was no time for a grave. No time for a goodbye. Just a quiet promise whispered as we shut the door behind us — a promise to make it matter.

The streets were different now.

Empty.

No growls. No screams. No movement in the windows or shadows. It was like the city had taken a breath and held it. Like the explosion — and Bryan's last stand — had drawn every infected thing in this part of hell to that single flashpoint.

Ash still floated through the air.

Burnt paper drifted down like snow. The sky was grey with smoke. Cars sat at odd angles, some with doors hanging open, others with shattered windshields. Every building we passed looked like a mouth waiting to open.

I caught myself glancing at the rooftops. Waiting for movement.

There was none.

CJ raised a hand and crouched at an intersection. We gathered around him. He pointed.

"One click south," he whispered. "Tunnel entrance behind the pharmacy. If it's not collapsed, we cut three miles off."

Charles scanned the windows. "We push fast. Stay tight. If it's too quiet, assume something's waiting."

We nodded. No argument. No wasted breath.

And we moved.

Step by step. Footfalls soft. Eyes sharp.

We passed scorched concrete and a blood trail dried into the road — possibly Bryan's. No one said it. But I felt Shaun linger on it.

The silence wasn't comforting.

It was pressure.

Like the city was watching.

Even CJ — normally full of sarcasm, even in hell — said nothing.

When we passed a wrecked school bus on the edge of the tunnel road, I noticed something in the window: a child's sneaker.

Still clean.

Untouched.

The others saw it too.

We didn't stop.

We kept walking.

And for the first time in a long time…

There were no dead.

Only ghosts.

The tunnel entrance was exactly where CJ said it would be.

Behind the pharmacy.

A rusted access gate, partially buried under collapsed concrete and twisted rebar, just wide enough to crawl through. The air around it was colder — stagnant and wet, like the city's lungs had collapsed.

CJ approached first, crouching near the entrance. "Looks like someone cleared it a while ago. Barricade's been pushed in."

Charles stepped forward, blade drawn. "That could mean survivors used it."

Shaun moved in closer, crouching low. He didn't say a word, just listened.

Then he froze.

The others noticed.

So did I.

Something was wrong.

Not quite — wrong.

There was sound… just not the kind we wanted.

It was subtle at first. A distant, wet clicking. Like bone tapping on stone. Then… the drag of something heavy across concrete. Then another sound — low breathing, not labored, not human, but heavy and *aware.*

CJ slowly rose from his crouch.

"Oh no…"

Shaun leaned in just far enough to get a glimpse inside.

And cursed under his breath.

"Back up."

"What is it?" I asked.

Shaun turned to me, jaw tight. "A nest."

I didn't understand at first.

Then the smell hit — thick rot and bile, deeper than anything we'd passed. And from inside the shadows… a *movement.* Dozens. Maybe more.

Figures.

Pale, twitching, clustered like insects, hunched along the walls and floor. Some were dragging their limbs in slow circles like they couldn't stand the silence. Others… others were standing perfectly still. Watching.

And one of them — bigger than the rest — was breathing through an open chest cavity like a second mouth.

Mutated.

Maybe three.

CJ backed up fast. "We're not going in there. We are *not* going in there."

Charles said nothing, but his eyes were locked on the blackness inside, like he was calculating if it could be done.

I looked again, and one of them twitched violently — a jerk of muscle like it had sensed us.

"They're asleep," Shaun said flatly. "Or something close to it."

CJ wiped his face. "We got eight miles left. This was supposed to cut it to five."

"I'm not dying in a hole full of twitching skin monsters," he added quickly.

Shaun didn't argue.

Charles stepped back from the entrance. "No one's going in that nest unless we've got fire. And we don't."

We stood there for a long moment, looking at the tunnel like it might breathe.

The only way forward…

Was now back into the open city.

Into exposure.

Into the unknown.

We were out of shortcuts.

We were backing away.

Quiet. Careful. Each step is like a loaded weapon.

The tunnel hadn't just been overrun. It had been claimed. Nesting ground for the infected. A hatchery of mutations.

We were maybe thirty feet from the mouth when it happened.

CJ stopped.

"Wait…"

Charles turned. "What?"

CJ slowly crouched and pressed two fingers to the pavement.

"It's warm."

Before anyone could speak—

A low, bone-deep growl rolled from inside the tunnel. Not a roar. Not a shriek. Something worse.

Intentional.

Then a noise that chilled my spine: a *series* of guttural *clicks*, timed like a pattern — not wild, not instinctual.

A signal.

Shaun's eyes widened. "We've been made."

From the dark, something massive moved.

It didn't lurch.

It didn't stumble.

It walked.

A hulking silhouette emerged from the shadows — nine feet tall, twisted, hunched but controlled. Its body was layered in armored bone, sinew stretched tight across its chest like dried leather. Its arms were long and deliberate, fingers extended and twitching like it was playing an invisible piano.

And its head…

Its skull was human. Elongated. Split vertically down the center, pulsing. No eyes. No nose. Just a faint *glow* in the seams — like something burned behind the bone.

Charles raised his knife. "Back. Now."

Shaun didn't move.

"It's not a drone," he said coldly. "It's the one giving the orders."

Behind the beast, movement stirred.

The entire nest began to shift — biters peeling from walls and ceiling like insects shedding from a hive. Crawling. Shuffling. Snapping their jaws in sync.

And then…

It raised one hand — long, jagged fingers curling inward.

And the entire swarm froze.

Hundreds of them.

Still.

Silent.

Waiting.

CJ whispered, "It's… It's controlling them."

"No," Charles muttered. "It's commanding them."

Then, with a single sharp motion, the thing pointed.

Straight at us.

The horde screamed to life.

Shaun grabbed my vest and shoved me back. "GO!"

We ran.

The sound behind us was biblical — dozens, maybe hundreds, of infected tearing through the streets like a tsunami of flesh and bone.

CJ pulled a flare from his vest and lit it, hurling it down a side alley.

"BUY SECONDS!" he yelled.

Charles turned and knocked over a trash bin, tossing his entire pack behind it — every last scrap of food, light, anything that could serve as a distraction.

"MOVE!" he bellowed.

We cut through the city ruins at a dead sprint, boots pounding over glass and wreckage. I didn't dare look back — not at the horde, not at the thing that led them.

But I heard it.

The clicking.

Faint at first, then louder, like teeth on steel.

It wasn't chasing.

It was guiding.

Not mindless.

Methodical.

The game had changed.

We weren't running from death anymore.

We were being hunted by intelligence.

12

FRACTURE LINE

We weren't a team anymore.

We were just people running.

There was no formation, no callsigns, no flawless movement. It was raw panic — boots slamming pavement, knives swinging wide, lungs burning with every step.

The tunnel was behind us, but the swarm it released was still coming. And worse… we knew now that it wasn't just a swarm. It was a strategy.

Charles yelled something — maybe "Left!" or "Cover me!" — but it was swallowed by the sound of claws scraping concrete and the thunder of the horde behind us.

CJ slashed at a biter that got too close, but it wasn't clean — his blade got stuck in its neck. Shaun tackled it to the ground and drove his own knife through the top of its skull, panting, blood dripping off his arm.

Charles cut down two in a blur, but his movements were rigid — no rhythm, no flow.

We were scattered.

Uncoordinated.

Terrified.

One of them came for me — fast. Too fast.

Its hands reached for my face, and I fired my pistol out of reflex — the last bullet in the mag. It missed. My ears rang.

I stumbled back, tripping over debris, and as the thing lunged again, I grabbed the brick near my foot and smashed it across its temple.

Once.

Twice.

Three times.

It collapsed, twitching.

I didn't stop.

Not until Charles pulled me back. "He's down! MOVE!"

I looked at my hand — blood all over it. My suit sleeve is torn. My breathing was ragged.

I'd killed things before.

But not like that.

CJ grabbed a fire extinguisher from a broken hallway and threw it at another infected trying to climb over a wrecked sedan. The impact shattered its jaw — Shaun followed with a knife to the throat, yelling without sound.

Even Shaun wasn't calm anymore.

We weren't Echo Black.

We were just the ones who hadn't died *yet*.

The infected kept coming in waves. We cut them down, but it wasn't surgical.

It was sloppy. Desperate. Wasteful.

And that clicking — that slow, deliberate clicking — was still out there, somewhere behind it all. Not chasing.

Just *watching*.

Directing.

CJ stumbled over a body and almost didn't get back up. Charles grabbed him by the collar and yanked him behind a broken wall, gasping. Shaun blocked a claw from scraping my leg and threw me into cover behind a collapsed mailbox.

I coughed hard. "We're falling apart!"

"No shit!" CJ snapped.

Shaun looked around, knelt beside me, and whispered, "We're not dying here."

His voice shook.

And that told me everything.

We had no ammo.

No clear path.

No coordination.

And no plan.

Only the fear of what we had just woken up.

The swarm wasn't thinning.

It wasn't breaking.

It was pressing — like a tide with no moon, flooding every alley, every path, every possible escape route we turned toward.

We moved as fast as we could, ducking into side streets and hopping over wreckage, but they were always just a step behind — snarling, shrieking, dragging the scent of blood behind them.

CJ yelled over the chaos, "There's a barricade ahead!"

Shaun veered left, throwing a rusted street sign into a cluster of infected just to buy us three seconds. Charles shoulder-checked a runner into a brick wall so hard that its skull collapsed.

We surged forward.

I was behind them — slower than I wanted to be, legs burning. I turned a corner too tight, clipped my shoulder against a jagged dumpster—

And that's when it grabbed me.

Cold fingers wrapped around my wrist.

Teeth tore into the back of my left hand.

I screamed.

It wasn't a lunge — it was intentional, like the damn thing *knew* where to strike.

I slammed it into the wall, but it held on like it wanted to rip my fingers off one by one. I bashed it again and again until its grip loosened, then drove my knife under its jaw, shaking.

Blood poured down my forearm.

The bite was deep. Bad. Obvious.

CJ turned and saw it. "NO—!"

Shaun froze mid-step. "Shit—President!"

I stumbled toward them, hand limp, blood soaking through my coat. "I'm fine—I'm—"

Charles ran to me and grabbed my wrist before I could even finish the sentence.

He looked at the bite.

Then looked into my eyes.

"Hold him," he said.

"What?!" I shouted.

"HOLD HIM DOWN!"

Shaun caught me from behind, arms around my chest.

"No—NO—"

Charles didn't wait.

He drew his machete in one clean, silent motion.

And brought it down.

CHUNK.

The pain didn't come first — it was the sound. The *wet snap* of bone. The heat. Then the shock. Then…

The scream.

My scream.

CJ ripped off his belt and tied the stump before I even realized I was on my knees.

Shaun held me up, shaking. His voice cracked. "You're good. You're *good*."

Charles knelt, grabbing the severed limb and tossing it into a trash fire as if it might still crawl. "We didn't have a choice."

I couldn't breathe. My vision was white at the edges.

But I was still here.

Hand gone. Mission intact.

"Keep moving," Charles said, standing. "They're still coming."

And they were.

Behind us, the clicking got louder.

The swarm hadn't stopped.

But I hadn't either.

We weren't Echo Black anymore.

We were fighting with teeth.

I was fading.

The pain wasn't sharp anymore — it was a throb, deep and bone-heavy. My entire body pulsed with it, like my heartbeat had moved into my shoulder. CJ's belt was still cinched around the stump of my wrist, sticky with blood and ash.

Each step was slower. Each breath is tighter.

I couldn't stop looking at my left side. My missing hand.

Gone.

Just like that.

Not in battle. Not to some grand act of bravery. I tripped. I got caught. And now… it was just gone.

My hand. The one I shook hands with foreign leaders. The one Emma used to hold at bedtime.

Now all I could hold was regret.

We stumbled into a construction lot filled with half-built towers — skeletal buildings of rebar and concrete. Empty scaffolding. Abandoned tools. A maze of unfinished progress.

Just like me.

Charles pushed ahead. Shaun covered the rear. CJ kept checking the map, as if it mattered. I just… followed. One leg at a time. My teeth clenched so hard I thought they'd break.

Who the hell was I now?

I wasn't a soldier. Wasn't a fighter. I was just on the mission. The package. A dying symbol held together by gauze and borrowed time.

My head was spinning.

Maybe they'd be better off if I just—

"DOWN!" Charles yelled.

Gunfire cracked through the street — but it wasn't at us.

A rope dropped in front of me, followed by a sudden whirring noise. I blinked, dizzy, confused.

Then a hook latched around my shoulder harness, and I was yanked upward.

"What the—"

A jolt of motion.

Shaun was pulled up next, followed by CJ, then Charles — one after the other. A camouflaged platform retracted into the wall of the unfinished building, sealing shut behind us as the horde flooded into the lot below.

But we were already gone.

The world flipped sideways.

We were inside… something.

A makeshift elevator shaft, repurposed with ropes and pulleys. The walls had soundproofing. Crates lined the floor. Traps had been rigged all across the lower levels.

Then I saw them.

People.

Not military. Not feral.

Survivors.

Two stood guard — both in scavenged gear, layered with welding masks and tactical pads. One had a modified nail gun. The other wore an apron splattered with paint — and blood.

An older woman stepped forward, maybe fifty, with dark skin, silver-streaked braids, and calm eyes. Real calm. The kind of calm you only get when you've survived everything.

"Tough break," she said, glancing at my stump.

I didn't answer.

She pointed to the couch. "Sit down before you pass out, hero."

I collapsed onto it, breath ragged, heart breaking.

"You live here?" CJ asked, still clutching his knife.

"For years," she said. "You just never noticed."

Charles narrowed his eyes. "How the hell are you still alive?"

"Because we didn't run," she said. "We adapted."

I barely heard her.

My vision blurred. My mind spiraled.

I couldn't feel my fingers anymore — because I had none.

I was the President of the United States.

And I had no idea who the hell I was now.

The moment we caught our breath, the questions came.

"Anyone bitten?"

It was fast. Sharp. No pity in the voice.

The older woman — the one who led this place — stood with her arms crossed, her eyes sweeping over us like she'd done it a hundred times. Not looking for answers. Looking for *truth*.

"No," CJ said immediately. "Not a scratch."

Charles didn't respond. His eyes shifted to me.

They followed.

Then the silence got heavy.

Shaun finally said it. "The President… got bit."

Guns didn't come up — but they didn't relax either.

"What the hell?" One of the guards took a step forward.

Charles raised a hand. "We handled it."

"How?" the woman asked.

Without a word, Charles walked to the nearest steel workbench, picked up a bent rebar with a flat edge, and placed it into the small furnace nearby — glowing orange with embers.

He nodded toward me. "CJ. Hold him."

My stomach dropped. "What—"

Charles didn't wait for approval.

CJ was already behind me. Shaun moved beside him.

"Wait—Wait—"

I started to rise, and Shaun pressed his hand against my chest. "We have to stop the bleeding. Or you won't wake up tomorrow."

Then Charles turned with the white-hot rebar.

I tried to move.

I couldn't.

I clenched my teeth. "Just do it."

The iron came down.

SIZZLE.

The pain hit like a tidal wave. My body went rigid, every nerve in my shoulder lighting up. The scream tore out of me before I even knew I was making it.

The smell was worse, like burning meat and metal, and fabric all at once. My flesh sealed shut, skin blackened, nerves ruined — but the blood stopped.

I collapsed back, soaked in sweat, breath shallow.

The woman nodded once. "Good call. Most wouldn't."

Charles didn't respond.

The guard with the nail gun exhaled. "Hell of a thing to do to your President."

"He's more than that now," Shaun muttered. "He's one of us."

We sat in silence for a few minutes while they distributed water, what little they had. They passed a bottle down the line. CJ gave me the first sip.

Then Charles spoke again.

"We need to know what that was. In the tunnel. The one that pointed at us."

The woman exchanged a look with one of her people.

"You saw it?"

Charles nodded. "It moved different. Controlled them. Like a general."

She sat down on a cinderblock stool, rubbing her fingers together like she'd been waiting for this moment.

"It's real," she said. "And it's worse than you think."

Shaun leaned in. "You've seen it before?"

The woman's eyes darkened. "Yeah. We call it… the Marrow."

CJ frowned. "Why?"

"Because it doesn't care about skin or blood or muscle. It *hollows them out*. Leaves just enough instinct to move… then replaces the rest with control. Like it drills into the bone."

Her voice dropped lower.

"It doesn't just lead them. It *guides* them. Shapes the horde. It studies. It waits."

Charles was quiet for a beat. "And it's building something in that tunnel."

She nodded. "A hive. Nest. Breeding ground — call it what you want. But it's growing. The infected that crawl out of there don't act like the others. They hunt in formations. They *set traps.*"

CJ stared at the floor, his voice hollow. "This thing's not a mutation. It's evolution."

"No," the woman said. "It's intention."

The room was still.

Then the guard with the apron spoke up. "By the way... sorry we can't offer much more. We used most of our ammo pulling you out. You brought half the city with you."

I nodded, still dazed from the cauterization, my voice raw.

"We didn't mean to."

The woman stood. "No one ever does... You can stay for a little while, but then you have

to leave.

Shaun looked at me. "You ready?"

I didn't answer.

Not yet.

We only got an hour.

That's what they told us — not kindly, not apologetically. Just matter-of-fact, like we were a leaky pipe they didn't want to deal with.

"You got sixty minutes," the woman said, tossing a cracked watch on the floor in front of Charles. "Then we expect you to be gone. We don't do charity. We don't do guests. We sure as hell don't do politics."

CJ scoffed. "We didn't ask for your help."

"And we didn't ask for a goddamn hornet's nest dragging its queen through our front door," she snapped back. "But here we are."

No one replied.

We were too tired to argue.

Their camp — if you could call it that — was cramped, fortified, and clearly designed to sustain only those who built it. Every hallway had bottlenecks, traps, and fallback zones. Their weapons were hand-welded hybrids. Their food was rationed, labeled, and counted.

Everything was about survival.

Just for them.

They weren't cruel. But they weren't allies. They weren't here to fight a war.

Just to make it to tomorrow.

CJ spread the map out on the floor again, running his finger along the streets.

"We're here," he muttered. "Sector 4C. Two blocks from the old civic center. Seven-point-two miles to extraction if we cut through the Ridge."

Charles sat with his back to the wall, blade across his lap. He looked like he hadn't blinked in ten minutes.

Shaun sat on the floor beside me, resting his head back, breathing through his mouth like he was trying not to pass out.

"I don't think I've slept in three days," he muttered.

"None of us have," CJ said. "But if we don't move soon, we'll be running from daylight and the next sweep."

I looked at my arm — or what was left of it. The pain was dulled now, but the exhaustion was worse. My whole body felt foreign. My breath felt shallow. My legs shook when I tried to stand.

"I'm slowing you down," I said.

"No," Charles replied instantly. "You're still the mission."

That shut me up.

A knock at the metal door broke the moment.

The guard in the apron peeked in. "If you're looking for ammo… there's a busted-up military van about three blocks west. Been there since the riots. Could be picked clean, but who knows."

Shaun raised an eyebrow. "Why tell us now?"

The man shrugged. "Because once you leave, you're not coming back."

CJ stood, rolled the map, and shoved it into his vest.

"That hour almost up?"

"Ten minutes," the guard said.

Charles rose like a mountain, stiff and silent.

Shaun pushed himself upright, groaning, blinking sleep out of his eyes.

I stood last. Slower. Leaner. One hand down, one mission left.

We were breaking. Bodies shot. Nerves raw.

But we were still moving.

Still together.

For now.

13

THIN VEIL

The door clanged shut behind us.

No farewell. No warning. Just the iron groan of rusted hinges slamming back into place — like a tomb sealing itself.

We were back in the open.

The air was thick with moisture, smoke still hung low in the sky, and the streets looked worse than they had when we ran in. But maybe that was just the weight behind our eyes. The blood was still caked on our sleeves. The hour we'd been given was enough to breathe, but not enough to recover.

It never was.

"Three blocks west," CJ muttered, checking the map under his breath. "Old riot zone. Grid 5 B. If that van's still there, it's sitting in a kill box."

"We don't have a choice," Charles replied. "Unless one of you knows how to make bullets out of broken promises."

Shaun didn't laugh. None of us did.

We moved like shadows — quiet, limping, tired.

The city had changed again. Quieter. But not safe. Not ever.

Windows stared at us like eyes. The wind moved through the streets like a whisper that couldn't decide if it was warning us or just waiting.

No infected.

Not yet.

But we'd seen how fast the Marrow could call them.

That thought never left my mind.

Neither did the pain.

I kept looking at my left arm — the stump wrapped in thick cloth and scorch lines. It wasn't bleeding anymore, but it pulsed like a second heartbeat. A reminder. Not just of what I'd lost… but what I still carried.

The cure.

Inside the pouch clipped to my chest. Closer to my heart now than my own blood.

I didn't know how long I could keep moving like this. But I knew one thing:

I had to.

For Bryan.

For Sheila.

For every goddamn person who didn't get to see the end of this.

Shaun suddenly raised a fist and crouched.

We all froze.

Ahead, just across the next intersection, nestled between a collapsed metro bus and a pile of concrete barriers, was the van.

Military green.

Heavily reinforced.

Wheels flat. Doors shut.

Still there.

Still whole.

CJ whispered, "Jackpot."

But none of us moved.

Because a jackpot usually meant a trap.

And we were too tired for another mistake.

We approached slow.

CJ circled wide, keeping low behind a burned-out sedan. Shaun covered our flank. I stuck behind them, my heart pounding with every step. The van didn't move. Didn't creak. Didn't give anything away.

But it felt wrong.

"Doors are shut," CJ whispered. "Glass is intact. No footprints nearby."

"That's not good," Shaun muttered.

Charles didn't speak. He just stepped forward, crouched near the rear wheel well, and inspected the ground. His fingers traced the dried blood splatter — old, but not ancient.

"This thing's been left untouched," he said, standing. "Which means everyone who saw it either didn't need it… or didn't make it."

He didn't have to say what we were all thinking:

Why's it still here?

CJ moved to the back. "I can pop the lock. No ignition. These old transport rigs ran on separate battery backups."

"Do it fast," Charles said. "If it's rigged, we find out now."

Shaun raised his knife and knelt by the passenger side. I stayed close to the wall of a busted storefront, my eyes bouncing between every shadow, every window.

CJ clicked open the rear door.

It opened with a creak.

No boom. No trigger.

Just the smell of old sweat, diesel, and rusted steel.

He slid the door wide — revealing the inside.

And for a second…

Hope.

Crates.

Sealed. Labeled. Government issue.

Shaun stepped inside and popped one open. "Water. Rations. First aid."

CJ cracked another. "Rounds. Nine mil. M4 mags."

Then Charles stepped past both of them and reached into the third crate — pulling out a loaded tactical belt and a radio pack.

He didn't smile.

But his eyes flicked to mine.

"We might have a shot."

For the first time in days…

It felt like something was turning.

But we didn't notice what else was turning…

Until it was too late.

For the first time in what felt like forever… There was hope.

Not a trickle. Not a desperate lie.

Real hope.

Water. Food. Ammunition. Medical kits still sealed. Rifles still oiled. Spare boots. Working batteries. The kind of supplies we used to take for granted—now the kind you bleed for.

CJ cracked open a pack of water bottles and held one up like it was a sacred relic. "Still cold."

Shaun opened a box of rations, pulled out a vacuum-sealed protein bar, and stared at it like he wasn't sure if it was real. "Tastes like crap, but it's our crap."

Charles moved through the gear silently, checking every corner. "This van's been parked here since before the fall," he muttered. "No sign of tampering. Doors weren't forced. Vitals intact."

I sat against the inside wall of the van, hand throbbing, arm weak—but my head was clearer than it had been in hours. For the first time since the blast, I let myself think:

We might actually make it.

CJ stepped into the cab and checked the glovebox. "Nothing weird. Just old papers. Fuel log. Maintenance records."

Shaun opened the passenger door to check under the seat—then stopped cold.

His voice dropped to a whisper. "Dad."

We turned.

He pointed to the far end of the intersection, past the van.

A figure stood in the shadow of a ruined overpass. Alone.

Pale.

Thin.

Lopsided gait.

Not a walker.

A scout.

Its head twitched unnaturally, neck bending in sharp clicks, like it had too many joints and no bones.

And its chest—

It breathed. Slow. Intentional. Controlled.

Shaun whispered, "That's not a normal infected."

Charles moved to the side door of the van, eyes narrowed. "No. That's one of his."

I knew who he meant before he said it.

The Marrow.

The figure just stood there, watching.

Not rushing.

Not shrieking.

Just memorizing us.

Then it turned—jagged, puppet-like—and started to retreat into the ruins.

CJ hissed, "It's going to call them."

"We kill it," Shaun said.

Charles shook his head. "No time. If it saw us, the call's already out."

I stood slowly, every breath harder than the last. "Then we need to move. Now."

Charles scanned the horizon. "We take what we can carry. No second trips."

Shaun loaded his pack. CJ grabbed ammo. I tucked trauma kits into my coat, strapping one over my shoulder with my remaining hand.

Then Charles turned to face us.

Voice cold. Commanding.

"From here on… we run."

They didn't come in waves this time.

They came in formation.

Like wolves — surrounding us.

Like soldiers — flanking us.

From the rooftop to the left, three infected vaulted across the gap like they were following orders. One dropped low, another darted wide. Their claws scraped against the pavement in sync.

From behind, another burst from a manhole, crawling on all fours before sprinting upright—silent, direct, eyes locked.

Shaun dropped one with a clean shot to the head, but the others didn't stop.

CJ shouted, "They're coordinating! They're boxing us in!"

"MOVE!" Charles bellowed, stepping in front of me. "Shaun, right flank! CJ, scatter run! Hector—stay on my six!"

A runner lunged toward me—too fast. I turned too slow.

Charles caught it mid-air, slammed it to the ground, and drove his boot through its skull without even breaking stride.

Blood sprayed his vest.

He didn't blink.

"WE MOVE ON MY CALL!"

We sprinted toward the alley to the east—what should've been clear—but the horde was waiting. Not charging. Waiting.

Charles paused mid-stride, breathing hard, reading the street like a battlefield.

"Diversion point," he growled.

Shaun tossed a flare over the cars into the far street. Nothing moved.

CJ reached for his second weapon, but Charles held up a hand. "No. Not yet."

The horde to our right started drifting.

Then stopped.

Then split.

Ten to one side. Fifteen the other. Cutting our only exit in half.

"They're funneling us," I said.

"No," Charles replied. "They're herding us."

Then, for the first time since I met him, I saw the real Viper Two — not the father, not the husband, not the sarcastic voice behind the rifle...

But the commander.

"Shaun," he barked. "Fire support west. Three-shot burst, ten-second interval. You see that armored one? Blind it."

"Copy."

"CJ—set flashbangs at the alley mouth. Space them six feet. Detonate on my mark."

"On it."

"Hector—you stick with me. Move when I move. No hesitation."

"Yes, sir."

Then Charles did something I didn't expect.

He smiled.

"That's more like it," he said, gripping his blade tighter.

Then the street erupted.

The infected charged — not like animals. Like units. Each movement is tight, fast, and overlapping. They didn't swarm.

They executed.

But Charles countered.

He moved like he'd trained for this exact moment — weaving through the chaos, calling out ranges, distances, impacts. Shaun's shots dropped targets in rhythm. CJ's detonations blasted open a pocket. Charles threw a smoke charge between two cars, grabbed my collar, and yanked me through the debris cloud before three biters could grab me.

We emerged on the other side — coughing, bleeding, alive.

Barely.

We could see the next street now — open, partially collapsed, but passable.

"THAT'S THE BREAK!" Charles yelled. "GO!"

We didn't hesitate.

We ran.

We didn't look back.

Not yet.

Because Charles was still behind us, buying seconds.

One command at a time.

They weren't just chasing us anymore.

They were herding us.

The infected came from behind in waves — but the side streets were already choked too. Every alley, every rooftop, every turn we made was met with snarling mouths and empty eyes.

This wasn't a collapse.

It was a maneuver.

"They're not funneling us," Charles growled as we ran. "They're boxing us."

"They're thinking like infantry," CJ panted. "Coordinated. Shifted lines. Some of them are feinting."

"Exactly," Charles said, steel in his voice. "The Marrow's not just leading. He's commanding."

Shaun fired three shots behind us. "Then how do we out-command a monster?"

Charles didn't break stride. "We outmaneuver it."

We turned a sharp corner, vaulted a fallen streetlight, and pushed into the ruins of an old drugstore. The glass crunched under our boots as we moved through the aisle. Charles scanned every shadow, every possible bottleneck, eyes calculating.

He didn't look tired.

He looked alive.

"Infected are converging east," CJ said, checking his watch. "Fifty seconds out, give or take."

Charles pointed toward the back. "We cut through the freezer aisle, cross through the alley, then head north into the parking structure. It's elevated, high ground—he can't funnel us as tight up there."

We moved fast. Sticking together. Every step coordinated.

But the sounds behind us — they weren't dying off.

They were growing smarter.

We burst into the alley behind the store and saw movement ahead — a small pack of biters climbing the same way we were trying to go. They weren't just shambling anymore. One was scaling the stair railing. Another moved with unnatural control in its limbs — stiff but efficient.

Charles charged first.

No hesitation.

He grabbed one by the collar and slammed it into the wall. The impact left a crater. His blade came down twice, fast, brutal. Shaun tackled another off the stairwell, stabbing with pure instinct. CJ stayed close to me, dropping one that got too close with a clean shot to the neck.

We pushed up the next flight.

More were coming.

Their screams were layered — high and low, some bone-chilling, others… almost organized like rows of them were shifting position around us.

"They're testing your routes," I said to Charles as we ran. "Adjusting to you in real time."

He didn't deny it.

He didn't slow down either.

"We'll change the rhythm," he said. "They can't keep up with unpredictability."

"How do you know that?"

He looked back once. Eyes burning. "Because I've led men into hell before — and I've seen what happens when the enemy forgets we still have teeth."

We reached the parking structure and slammed the gate shut behind us. It wouldn't hold for long — but it bought seconds.

CJ gasped, wiping sweat off his face. "We're bleeding time."

"Then we don't waste it," Charles said. "We bait the push, and when the next opening hits, we move as one. No splitting. No heroes. We fight through and make distance."

He scanned the next level, looking for bottlenecks, structure, and movement. "We stick together. We stay alive."

And just like that, even surrounded by monsters with strategy, with Marrow's eyes closing in, we believed him.

Because Charles believed.

Because in that moment, he wasn't just leading.

He was already sacrificing pieces of himself to get us through.

And none of us noticed…

How much quieter he'd gone.

We were running out of stairs.

CJ was firing over the rail as we climbed. Shaun held the rear, slashing through anything that got close. The stairwell was collapsing behind us — screams, cracking steel, and the thundering rise of bodies that weren't supposed to be this fast.

"Third landing!" Charles barked. "Go! Don't stop!"

The air was thick — smoke, blood, sweat — like the world itself was trying to choke us out before we ever reached the top.

Then, just as we reached the final door, Charles stopped.

He didn't speak.

No final speech.

No dramatic pause.

Just a single moment — quiet, brutal.

He reached up, tore the chain from his neck, and shoved his dog tags into my hand.

Hard.

His eyes locked with mine.

Not begging. Not explaining.

Just goodbye.

And before I could say anything — before Shaun could yell or CJ could question — Charles kicked open the door and led us into the storm.

We hit the rooftop in full sprint.

And hell was already waiting for us.

The concrete was cracked and glowing under patches of fire. Infected swarmed the sides, crawling over the edge like spiders. The wind screamed across our skin. The sky above us burned orange.

We didn't even have time to find cover.

Because he was already there.

The Marrow emerged from the smoke like it had been waiting all along. Its body was wrong — shifting in ways that didn't make sense. Limbs too long. Head pulsing faintly with an inner glow, like something alive was inside its skull.

It moved faster than anything that big should move.

And it went straight for Charles.

It tackled him mid-sprint, slamming into him with such force that the metal beneath them buckled.

They crashed into the far railing — and in a single, violent moment, they were gone, tumbling off the edge.

"DAD!" Shaun screamed, sprinting after them.

CJ screamed, "NO!"

We all ran to the edge — but there was only smoke and distance.

No sign of him.

And then—

The comms crackled.

Charles' voice came through, low and ragged. Fighting. Bleeding. Still giving orders.

"This is Viper Two—engaged with the primary."

Gunfire burst behind his voice. Wet sounds. Bone snapping. Roars.

"This thing—this thing is the hive. You kill it, you end this."

We could hear the struggle. Something slammed. He coughed. Breathed hard. Gritting his teeth through whatever was tearing into him.

"CJ—listen to me. You were always smarter than I. Now prove it. Finish what I couldn't."

"Shaun…"

His voice cracked.

"You're not a weapon. You're my son."

"Keep your brother safe. And don't ever let this world change who you are."

And then—

A whisper, like he knew we'd hear it even if he didn't say it loud.

"Tell your mother I never stopped fighting for her."

A final gunshot.

A final scream.

And then—

Silence.

Just static.

Shaun collapsed at the railing, hands in his hair, shaking. CJ stood frozen, gun limp at his side. I clutched the dog tags like they were the only proof he'd ever existed.

He was gone.

And the world didn't even pause to grieve.

ASH AND TEETH

The rooftop was a grave waiting to happen.

Smoke, screams, and the thunder of infected crashing over the ledges. The stairwell behind us was gone — swallowed in bodies. Blood slicked the concrete. Fire cracked in the distance.

Charles was gone.

And we were still breathing.

But not for long.

An infected charged me from the right.

I couldn't raise my pistol — the clip was empty.

I couldn't brace — not without my left hand.

So I let it come.

And at the last second, I pivoted and drove my knife into its side with my remaining hand. The impact spun me — hard — but I stayed on my feet. The thing shrieked as I twisted the blade and kicked it off me, stumbling back against a broken pipe.

Shaun's voice cut through the noise.

"He gave you the tags?!" CJ shouted at him, his knife already soaked.

Shaun parried a wild claw and drove his blade under a biter's jaw. "What does it matter?!"

CJ slashed another across the throat, stepping in close. "Because I was the one with him—I was the one right behind him—he didn't even look at me!"

"I didn't ask for them!"

"He should've said goodbye!"

"He shouldn't have had to!"

A screecher crawled over the northern ledge — I grabbed a steel rebar chunk off the floor with my one good arm and swung hard, catching it across the temple. It fell sideways, cracking against the railing, motionless.

I grunted. My legs were shaking.

CJ screamed as he fought. "You think it's easier because you got his last words?!"

Shaun drove his knife through another and yanked it out with a breathless roar. "It doesn't make anything easier! It makes it worse!"

Their pain was spilling out mid-fight. Grief swinging wild with every blow.

And we were barely holding the line.

I dropped another infected by grabbing its collar with my elbow and slamming my knife into its heart — clumsy, unbalanced, but fast.

One hand. One weapon. No choice.

CJ wiped blood from his eyes. "He should've let one of us do it—should've let me go!"

"He wouldn't let either of us," Shaun snapped. "Because you'd both be dead!"

"He still left!"

Shaun's eyes flashed. "To save us."

I pulled the dog tags from my jacket and stared at them for a single breath.

They felt heavier now. Like they knew we were breaking.

Without a word, I shoved them back into the inside pocket and turned to the boys.

"We finish this."

I raised my knife again, panting. "I'm not burying anyone else."

A new wave hit the rooftop edge.

No time for grief.

No time for healing.

Just three broken men…

Still fighting.

Still alive.

Because he wasn't.

We didn't run.

We fled.

There was no plan, no order — just instinct and fire and falling concrete.

CJ spotted the damaged scaffolding on the far end of the roof — rusted, bent, barely holding against the side of the building.

"That's our drop!" he shouted.

Shaun didn't argue. He didn't even breathe. He grabbed my vest and pushed me toward it.

We ran, blades dripping, lungs burning.

Behind us, the infected still poured through the stairwell like a wave with no ocean, aimless but relentless.

CJ reached the scaffold first, testing it with a hard stomp.

"Don't look down," he muttered. "Just move."

Shaun dropped into position second. Then me.

I had to lower myself with one hand — the other was gone. Burned, bandaged, dead weight. I gritted my teeth, balanced my knife in my mouth, and slid.

The whole structure groaned under our weight.

Metal warped.

The bolts squealed.

Halfway down, part of the railing gave out behind us.

CJ didn't stop moving. Shaun didn't stop checking over his shoulder.

I didn't stop bleeding.

We hit the alley hard and didn't pause. The buildings around us were collapsing — not from explosives, not from rot, but from time. From the weight of a city that had died screaming.

We cut across the cracked pavement, slipped between the shells of patrol cars, and dodged a bus skeleton still smoldering. The infected didn't follow in a wave now — they came in spurts, uncoordinated, shrieking like animals sniffing blood but unsure where to strike.

Shaun stabbed one in the neck and kept moving.

CJ kicked another into a crater of broken asphalt.

I limped. Focused. Knife still wet in my one good hand.

We kept running.

Street signs were scorched beyond recognition. Windows were blown out. We moved through open homes, ruined markets, dead intersections—each step burning deeper into our legs.

No time to rest.

No time to grieve.

Only four miles.

Four miles between us and extraction.

Between us and the reason Charles died.

We reached a blown-out gas station and stopped inside the shadow of the awning. Our breaths were shallow. Our bodies are barely holding together.

CJ checked the compass and looked west. "Four miles. If the streets are still open… we can make it by dusk."

Shaun nodded slowly, wiping blood off his blade. "We make it."

He didn't say for Dad.

He didn't have to.

I pulled the dog tags from my jacket and stared at them in the fading light.

Then I looked at both of them.

Four miles to go.

One chance left.

We didn't have a plan.

We had a direction.

And that was enough.

We found a place to fall apart.

A caved-in lobby, half its ceiling gone, dead office furniture scattered across the floor like bones. No infected. No fire.

Just us.

CJ leaned against a cracked filing cabinet, fists balled at his sides. Shaun sat with his back against the wall, head low, arms on his knees, eyes fixed on the floor.

No one spoke.

Not for a while.

Until CJ finally broke.

"You're just… sitting there?"

Shaun didn't answer.

CJ pushed off the cabinet, pacing hard, teeth grinding. "You haven't said a word. Haven't even looked at me. Like it didn't happen."

Shaun's jaw tensed. "What do you want me to say?"

CJ turned, voice sharp. "That it hurts. That it ripped something out of you."

Shaun's voice was quieter, colder. "I'm not gonna fall apart in front of you."

CJ barked a bitter laugh. "Right. Because falling apart is weak. Because showing anything means you're not the one holding the line."

"I didn't say that."

"You didn't have to."

Shaun stood now. Not aggressive—just tired. Torn.

"You think this is easy for me?"

CJ stepped forward. "You're not showing anything, Shaun."

Shaun shook his head slowly. "Because if I do, I won't stop."

CJ blinked. "Then maybe you should. Just for a second. Just let it fucking hurt."

Shaun turned away, hand to his face. "I watched him fall."

CJ's voice cracked. "We both did."

Shaun wiped his face, then clenched his fists. "And we kept moving. Because if we stopped—we'd die. He knew that."

CJ turned, putting a hand to the wall, leaning into it. "I don't know how we keep doing this without him."

And there it was.

Not anger.

Not blame.

Just the hole that man left behind.

And it was swallowing us.

I stepped in.

I was done waiting for the storm to pass. I stepped between them, bloody, shaking, one hand still clenched around my blade. I looked at both of them — not like soldiers.

Like sons.

"He's not coming back," I said.

CJ's eyes welled again.

Shaun didn't meet mine.

"And none of us got to choose who the Marrow took," I continued. "None of us has time to prepare for it. That's what war does. It steals people and leaves you nothing but silence."

I pulled out the dog tags and held them between us.

"I was there. He didn't hesitate. He knew what he was doing. He bought you four more miles. Four more chances to make this mean something."

Shaun looked up, face hollow. "He would've led us through all of it."

"No," I said. "He would've gotten you here. Just like he did."

CJ covered his face, his voice ragged. "He was everything."

"And now," I said softly, "he's part of why we're still breathing."

They didn't speak again.

Not right away.

Shaun sat down. CJ slumped against the wall.

I sat with them.

And for just a few minutes… we let it hurt.

Shaun sat against the far wall, elbows on his knees, head down, eyes hollow.

CJ slumped nearby, leaning against a snapped support beam, arms wrapped over his midsection like holding himself together was the only thing left he could control.

The silence wasn't peaceful.

It was just quiet enough to feel the emptiness.

I stood.

Still bleeding. Still broken. But standing.

My legs ached. My balance was uneven. My missing hand pulsed with dull, hateful heat.

But I had something inside me now I hadn't had since this started.

Resolve.

Because for so long, I'd been just the thing they were protecting. The responsibility that got people killed. The cure in a suit.

But Charles didn't throw himself into death for the cure.

He did it for me.

I took a breath and let my voice fill the room.

"I know what I've been to you."

Neither of them looked at me.

CJ's eyes stayed locked on the floor. Shaun's stare was somewhere far past the ruined window behind me.

"The mission. The cure. The reason to keep walking. And the reason some of you… don't get to anymore."

Their faces didn't move.

But I saw the truth in their silence.

I stepped closer.

"He died for me," I said. "Not for what's in my pocket. For me. And I've spent every mile behind him… behind all of you… surviving while you bled."

Shaun blinked slowly, face unreadable.

CJ's shoulders rose just a little.

"And I'm done being dead weight."

I dropped to one knee beside them — low, grounded, eye level. My left arm is useless. My right hand was still gripping the knife that had saved me more times than I could count.

"I'm walking the rest of the way with you. Not behind. Not guarded. Not carried."

I held the knife in front of me.

"I may not be a soldier. I may not be your father. But I'm not a package anymore."

I glanced between them.

"And I'm not leaving this city unless it's on my own two feet."

Shaun looked at me — not the same blank stare as before.

CJ finally raised his head, jaw trembling but nodding once.

We didn't say Charles' name.

We didn't have to.

I reached into my coat and gripped the dog tags. They were still warm.

Still with us.

"Make the President a person. Not a package."

Then I stood.

And this time…

They followed.

The second we stepped out of that ruined office building, the silence changed.

It wasn't peace anymore.

It was pressure.

Like the city had been holding its breath… and just remembered we were still inside it.

We moved fast.

There was no more hesitation. No more breaking down.

We were four miles from extraction.

No more Charles.

No more backup.

Just us.

CJ reloaded beside me, slapping in a fresh mag. "Two full, one half," he muttered.

Shaun checked his belt. "Same here."

I reached into my coat and pulled my pistol from its holster — my right hand still trembling from the adrenaline, my left a memory. I cracked it open, slid in the last rounds I had left.

Six bullets.

That's all I had between me and a corpse.

CJ glanced at me as we stepped into the street. "You sure you can still shoot with one hand?"

I gave a humorless smile. "I've got six chances to find out."

Shaun kept his eyes forward. "Don't waste any of them."

We moved in a tight formation — not like a military unit, not anymore.

Like a family that had nothing left to lose.

The buildings on either side were twisted, leaning in like dying trees. Glass crunched beneath our boots. The wind carried rot. Somewhere far off, something metal fell — a clatter in the distance, like the city warning us not to relax.

We didn't speak.

We didn't breathe easy.

We just kept moving.

One block passed. Then two.

Every step felt like a countdown.

CJ was first to say what we were all feeling.

"It's too quiet."

Shaun didn't look back. "That's what scares me."

Because the horde hadn't come back.

The infected weren't screaming in the distance.

No footsteps. No shrieks.

Just tension.

Something was coming.

Something that didn't need noise to hunt.

I checked the pistol again. Six rounds. One hand. Four miles.

I wasn't the same man I was at the start of this.

And whatever was waiting for us…

It was going to find out fast that I wasn't just a passenger anymore.

SOMETHING SEES US

We saw it too late.

At first, it looked like a shadow — just movement behind shattered windows on the far end of the street. A flicker. A glitch in the silence. CJ froze mid-step, eyes narrowing.

"Hold."

We stopped.

The air went still.

Then we saw it clearly.

Another scout.

Thin. Twitchy. Its head tilted unnaturally sideways like a puppet held up by an invisible string. No snarl. No sound. Just that same slow, calculating movement like the one that had spotted us before.

It didn't run.

It didn't charge.

It simply stared.

Shaun stepped forward. "Take it down—"

"Too late," CJ snapped. "It's already seen us."

And then—

It screamed.

Not a roar. Not a shriek.

A signal.

The sound tore through the air like a rip in the sky — high-pitched, vibrating, unnatural.

CJ's voice dropped to a whisper. "Get ready."

Then came the noise.

Not footsteps.

Thunder.

Two hundred strong. Maybe more.

A tidal wave of flesh and rot and fury, sweeping toward us from every direction.

We weren't being hunted.

We were being crushed.

It didn't feel like a fight.

It felt like drowning in fists and teeth.

The street cracked beneath us as the first wave slammed in — snarling, sprinting, biting, mindless chaos with one goal: to tear us apart.

CJ fired point-blank into the chest of a runner and spun to reload without missing a beat.

Shaun was already moving — ducking, slicing, stabbing, each motion clean and fast. His knife found eyes. Throats. Arteries. His blade sang through flesh.

"Left flank!" CJ shouted.

Shaun didn't even respond — he was already there, dropping two biters before they touched the pavement.

They weren't brothers now.

They were a machine.

Fluid. Deadly.

Everything Sheila ever said they were true.

I slammed my shoulder into an infected that got too close, sending it tumbling into a broken post. My pistol came up — six rounds.

I fired three.

One missed.

Two didn't.

"BACK!" CJ shouted. "Behind the wrecked sedan — bottleneck them!"

We moved. Fast. Tight. No hesitation.

The sedan had flipped onto its side near the corner of the street— rusted out, engine block still leaking black. We pressed against the frame, forcing the horde to come at us in one direction only.

It helped.

But not enough.

They kept coming.

Over the tops of cars. Through shattered store windows. Around, over, under.

CJ dropped his last mag into his rifle. "One left!"

Shaun knifed an infected in the chest, twisted, and pulled it into another charging from the right — using its body like a meat shield before driving the knife into both.

"They're folding in!" Shaun growled. "We have maybe three minutes!"

CJ looked to him — not afraid. Not shaken.

Just ready.

"You thinking what I'm thinking?"

Shaun nodded. "You go high. I go low."

And they moved.

Together.

CJ vaulted the car, landed clean, and tackled two biters into the concrete, firing as he went. Shaun ducked under a swing and hamstrung an infected so fast that it collapsed screaming.

One after another.

Precise. Brutal.

Perfect.

Sheila's voice echoed in my memory — her last quiet praise before she died.

"When they work together, nothing touches them."

I believed it now.

I turned, three rounds left, and fired into a sprinter charging CJ's blindside.

It dropped inches from him.

CJ gave a sharp nod. "Thanks."

Shaun kicked a corpse off his knife. "He's not cargo anymore."

I looked at the storm around us.

And I realized—

Neither were they.

They were fire.

And everything around them was burning.

We weren't winning.

We were enduring.

The first wave collapsed under our feet — bodies stacked in the street like sandbags, blood pooling in every crack of the pavement. But the sound didn't stop.

The ground shook again.

The second wave was already coming.

And it was worse.

Bigger infected. Faster. Their screams didn't echo — they drowned everything.

Shaun grunted as he ripped his knife free from a chest, his arms twitching with exhaustion. "They just keep coming—!"

CJ fired the last rounds from his final mag, pulled the bolt, and tossed the rifle aside. "That's it—I'm dry!"

I was down to one bullet.

One.

My hands were slick with blood — not all of it mine. My shoulder throbbed. My legs felt like rebar. But I kept moving. Because stopping meant dying.

CJ switched to his sidearm and kicked open the door of a burned-out corner shop. "Funneled entrance — take them here!"

We rushed in, climbing over debris, using shelves for cover. Shaun dropped low and slashed at the ankles of the first biter that came through — it screamed, fell, and he drove his blade into the side of its face with a growl.

He didn't speak anymore.

None of us did.

Our lungs were done with words. We just fought.

I smashed a bottle against the side of a crawling infected and shoved glass into its neck with my bare fingers. CJ crushed another with a fire extinguisher he found behind the register. Shaun grabbed a fallen pipe and went to work like a man possessed.

They were tiring.

Slower now.

CJ's swings got heavier. Shaun's steps dragged. Every stab took a second longer. My knife kept getting stuck in some zombies neck and I almost didn't have the strength to pull it free.

The horde didn't care.

It just kept coming.

They slipped over the counters, clawed through broken glass, shoved their own corpses aside like trash.

CJ blocked the door. Shaun guarded the back wall.

I stood between them — a bleeding, one-handed President with a knife, a bullet, and a promise.

CJ locked eyes with me. "We're getting boxed."

Shaun's voice was hoarse. "Too many. They're choking us."

My hand shook on the grip of my pistol.

I looked to the front, to the bodies piling up.

And then I heard something...

Low.

Subtle.

But different.

Not a scream.

Not a growl.

Not infected.

A breath.

Just beyond the glass.

Watching.

We were seconds from breaking.

CJ's blade clashed against bone. Shaun's breath came in gasps, his arms trembling from strain. I had nothing left but a knife and shaking legs. The street was flooding with them again — screaming, snarling, teeth bared.

And then—

One shot.

Clean.

A runner's skull snapped back in mid-lunge, folding like paper.

Then another.

And another.

Sharp, surgical. From somewhere high above.

Shaun paused mid-swing. "Sniper?!"

CJ turned toward the rooftops, blinking through the smoke.

And then—

The comms lit up.

"This is Viper Two. I've got eyes on you."

Shaun froze.

CJ's mouth dropped. "Dad—?"

"Don't talk. Don't stop. I'm giving you a corridor — now MOVE!"

The rifle cracked again — perfect. The biter about to flank CJ crumpled, lifeless.

We bolted. No hesitation.

Every few steps, a clean shot dropped another threat. Charles was clearing the path with terrifying precision.

But the truth was bleeding through his voice.

"South alley. Cut through the yellow scaffolding. Don't slow down."

CJ fumbled through debris, nearly slipping. "We can reach you—"

"Negative." Charles' voice was ragged now. "I'm hit bad. Bleeding out. Left arm's gone below the shoulder."

Shaun stopped for a beat.

Just a beat.

"I'm boxed in. High rise. Fifth floor, northeast sector. I've got two, maybe three minutes before they reach me."

CJ's voice broke. "We can get up there. We can still—"

"NO!" Charles barked.

Silence.

Then his voice came again.

"You don't come back for me."

"You survive. You hear me? You. Fucking. Survive."

Shaun's eyes brimmed — the blade in his hand trembled now. "Dad…"

"I don't need goodbyes. I need you to finish this."

"Boys, listen closely. I'm proud of you, always have been. Sorry to have to say goodbye this way, Charles chuckled. STAY STRONG AND SHOW THEM THAT ECHO BLACK ALWAYS COMPLETES THE MISSION NO MATTER WHAT."

CJ dropped behind a ruined post, sobbing now, eyes wide, whispering "No no no no—"

"Mr. President…"

I stopped. Swallowed. My throat was tight. "Charles…"

"Get them out."

"They're yours now."

One more shot cracked.

Then another. Closer this time.

The radio hissed — we heard him grunt, then a burst of movement, shuffling, a rifle shifting position.

"They're breaching. This is Viper Two out."

We kept running.

Through blood, smoke, and tears.

Shaun is in front.

CJ is beside me.

And behind us — unseen, dying, and still fighting —

Viper Two never missed a shot.

THE ROAD BLEEDS BEHIND US

We didn't speak for the first half-mile.

Not one word.

We just moved.

Down shattered alleyways, through broken streets soaked in old blood and ash, with Viper Two's voice still in our ears like a phantom we weren't ready to silence.

Every gunshot from above.

Every command.

Every word he gave us.

Echoed.

CJ's hands were shaking, his face pale, but his steps didn't falter. He led like someone trying not to collapse in front of the only thing that mattered: his brother.

Shaun was dead silent. Eyes forward. Knife still clutched tight. Every breath came low and deep, like he was saving strength for the next fight.

And I was behind them.

Knife drawn. One hand. Still bleeding. Still alive.

The weight of Charles' dog tags pressed into my chest with every step.

We passed an overturned ambulance, a church with one steeple still burning, and the skeletal remains of what used to be a barricade line — now just rusted metal and shredded riot shields.

CJ finally spoke.

"Two miles."

Shaun nodded once. "We don't stop."

We didn't.

But every step we took…

The city watched.

The wind was picking up.

Smoke rolled low over the cracked streets as we moved in a triangle — tight, deliberate, heads on a swivel. No one ran. We didn't have the strength for that anymore.

But we moved fast enough to matter.

CJ checked his vest and muttered, "I'm dry. Bone-dry."

Shaun didn't look back. "Same."

I reached for my pistol — nothing but weight.

I nodded. "Me too."

CJ let out a bitter laugh. "Hell of a time to run out."

Shaun's voice was flat. "Not like it's new."

CJ adjusted the makeshift wrap on his arm and kicked a rock off the road. "We're two miles from extraction, no ammo, no backup, and the city wants us dead."

Shaun finally looked at him. "Then we don't give it what it wants."

They locked eyes. Nothing angry in it. Just grief underneath steel.

I slowed my pace for a moment and said quietly, "You know… I've been dead weight for most of this."

CJ looked back, frowning. "Don't."

"I mean it," I said. "Your dad… Sheila… Bryan... They didn't die to save a cure. They died to save me."

Shaun's jaw tightened. "They didn't die for you."

I stopped walking.

He turned.

"They died for the mission," he said. "They died because they believed in something more than just making it out. That doesn't make you a burden. That makes you the reason it mattered."

CJ wiped his eyes with the back of his hand, quickly. "He's right."

I didn't argue.

We started walking again.

Shaun whispered, "You're one of us now."

And for a few quiet seconds, I believed him.

Then—

A distant screech.

Low.

Inhuman.

We all stopped.

CJ turned, blade raised. "Left."

Shaun scanned the rooftops. "They're regrouping."

I felt the shift in the air.

We weren't done.

Not yet.

It started with a sound.

A deep, wet growl that didn't echo — it just hung in the air, like it didn't care if we heard it.

CJ was first to move. "Eyes up—"

The thing dropped from a half-collapsed balcony above us before the sentence finished. Eight feet tall. Its arms are too long. Its skin stretched thin across what used to be muscle. But its eyes… those were still human.

And angry.

CJ didn't get to react. It slammed into him mid-step, full force, and drove him into the pavement so hard the ground cracked.

He didn't even scream.

Just collapsed.

"CJ!" Shaun shouted.

But the thing was already turning toward us.

Shaun was on it in a heartbeat — blade-first, full sprint, rage pouring off him like heat. He slammed into the mutant's side and drove the knife into its ribs, twisting hard. It screamed, grabbing Shaun by the vest and hurling him backwards against a crushed traffic sign.

I dropped beside CJ. He was breathing. Bleeding. But unconscious.

I checked his pulse. Fast. Shallow.

The mutant turned toward me next.

But Shaun roared back, dragging a chunk of rebar from the sidewalk and rushing it again.

I had one job.

Keep CJ alive.

I grabbed his body under the arms and dragged him behind the wreckage of an overturned car. The metal burned my hands. My legs trembled. But I didn't stop.

Shaun was a monster now — not infected, not changing — but fighting like something wild. He ducked the mutant's next swing and drove the rebar into its knee. It howled, staggered, and swiped again. Shaun caught the hit with his shoulder and didn't flinch.

He stabbed.

Again.

And again.

Until it stopped moving.

Then the screams came.

Different ones.

Dozens.

From the south alley. From rooftops. From open sewer grates.

A horde.

A real one this time.

I propped CJ's limp body against the car and stood, blade in hand, breathing like fire was in my chest. "Shaun…"

He was already turning toward the noise. Blood in his teeth. Clothes torn. Knife raised.

"They're coming," I said.

Shaun nodded. "Then we stop them here."

"They'll tear us apart."

Shaun glanced down at CJ. Then back at me.

"Not before I do first."

And then he moved.

Straight into the alley mouth — where the first dozen were already running, full speed.

He hit them head-on.

No time to think.

No space to breathe.

Just motion, steel, blood.

I crouched by CJ and shielded him with my body.

I couldn't help Shaun.

I couldn't stop what was coming.

But I could make sure CJ didn't die alone.

And from the street—

Through the screams—

I still heard Shaun.

Grunting.

Slashing.

Roaring.

Fighting like someone who knew this might be the last time he ever did.

The alley was red.

Blood ran in streams down the cracked concrete — infected, human, we couldn't tell anymore.

Shaun was a storm in the middle of it.

One blade.

Two dozen enemies.

His arms were cut. His shirt was soaked. His jaw locked as if he let it go, he'd scream himself apart.

But he never stopped moving.

He kicked the legs out from under a biter, dropped to one knee, and drove his knife upward into its throat in one motion. He pivoted, slashed another across the face, spun, ducked, stabbed.

But they were endless.

And every second he fought…

I was crouched behind the wrecked car, blade in hand, back against CJ — still unconscious, still not waking.

Until they came for him.

Two infected. Smaller. Faster. Runners.

They peeled off from the group chasing Shaun, sensing a softer target.

I stood fast.

One hand.

No time.

I met the first one mid-charge and slammed it into the hood of the car, jamming my knife into its eye before it even screamed. The second lunged from the side, caught my shoulder, and knocked me down—

But I kicked.

Hard.

It stumbled, and I stabbed upward from the ground, carving open its chest.

CJ groaned behind me.

I turned fast.

"CJ—wake the hell up."

He blinked.

Then gasped.

Eyes wide, chest heaving.

"Where—Shaun—?!"

I pointed to the alley.

He sat up just in time to see his brother fighting alone — surrounded, soaked in blood, staggering now.

Shaun let out a hoarse roar and tackled a biter to the ground. Another clawed his back. He shook it off. Swung wild.

CJ started to move, but too late—

Shaun screamed.

Just once.

A deep, guttural cry.

CJ froze. "No—"

I saw it.

A biter latched onto Shaun's side, buried into his ribs.

Shaun grabbed its head and ripped it off him, throwing the corpse into another and stabbing it before it hit the ground.

He stood.

Bleeding.

Panting.

Still fighting.

But now — bitten.

And CJ just stood there.

Staring.

Shaking.

"No…"

And Shaun looked at him—

Blood running from his waist.

Eyes full of fire.

And kept swinging.

CJ reached him before I did.

He sprinted past the wreckage, skidded through the blood, and grabbed Shaun by the shoulder just as his knees started to give out.

Shaun batted him off with one arm. "I'm fine."

His voice was hoarse. Hollow.

CJ ignored him. "Let me see it."

"No."

"Shaun—"

"I SAID NO."

Shaun took a step back, panting, clutching his side with his free hand. His shirt was soaked through. The wound still bled — deep, ragged, unmistakable.

CJ's voice cracked. "You're… you're bit."

Shaun's eyes met his, and for a second—just a second—he looked like the kid brother again. Not the knife-wielding soldier. Not the man who took on the world. Just the boy who used to follow CJ through the woods behind their house.

He didn't say yes.

He didn't have to.

CJ staggered back, like the words had hit him harder than the mutant earlier.

"No. No, no—"

Shaun grabbed him. "Hey. Look at me."

CJ's chest heaved. "We're not doing this again."

"Then don't."

"We're not losing you too. We're not—we can figure it out—there's a cure on your chest!" He turned to me, eyes wild. "Tell him! There's a goddamn cure!"

I couldn't speak.

The words were there.

But the air wasn't.

Shaun turned toward me, his hand still pressed to the bite. "Is it true?"

I nodded. Slowly. "Yes."

He looked down at the blood staining his fingers.

Then back at me.

"But it's not for me, is it?"

I didn't answer.

He already knew.

CJ dropped to his knees in the blood. "We should've gone back for him. We should've brought Dad with us."

Shaun crouched beside him, wincing through the pain.

"He brought us here," Shaun said. "He's the reason we made it this far."

CJ shook his head. "And now—now you're gonna—"

"I'm not dead yet."

CJ looked up, eyes red. "But you will be."

Shaun looked toward the skyline.

The clouds were darker now.

The wind is colder.

Extraction was close.

But time? Time was running out.

TWO MILES TO GOODBYE

We moved in silence.

The city didn't scream anymore.

No wind. No horde. Just dust in the air and our footsteps, soft and tired, echoing down cracked asphalt and hollow buildings.

Two miles left.

And Shaun was still walking.

But it was slower now.

A little more weight in every step.

He kept behind us. Said nothing about it.

But we felt it.

CJ glanced back the third time in five minutes. Didn't say anything. Just stared at his brother — jaw clenched, eyes wet, chest tight.

I could feel it in the space between us.

The way Shaun winced when he stepped. The way his right hand hovered near the bite like he couldn't help touching it. His knuckles were white around the handle of his blade.

He was still fighting.

But not the infected anymore.

Just the time left in his blood.

CJ finally slowed, letting the distance close.

"Hey," he said softly. "You good?"

Shaun didn't answer right away. He kept walking, slower now.

Finally, he said, "Hurts."

CJ swallowed. "How bad?"

Shaun chuckled under his breath — dry, broken. "Feels like something's eating me from the inside. So… probably what you'd expect."

CJ stopped walking.

I turned around in time to see Shaun stop beside him.

CJ whispered, "We can rest. Just for a second."

Shaun looked at him. Really looked.

And shook his head.

"I don't wanna stop. Because if I stop, I don't think I'll start again."

CJ's mouth opened — closed — opened again.

Nothing came out.

Shaun patted his shoulder. "Don't look at me like that."

CJ blinked fast. "Like what?"

Shaun smiled — small, quiet, knowing.

"Like you already see a ghost."

I didn't say anything.

There wasn't a word in the world I could give them.

I just turned, gripped the handle of my knife, and started walking again.

A little slower this time.

So he wouldn't fall too far behind.

The sky had gone gray.

Not storm gray — just the dull, dead haze of a city that had forgotten what sunlight was. It cast a colorless light over everything: bone-white buildings, ash-covered roads, blood that looked more like rust now.

We moved quietly.

Shaun stayed with us.

But it was like watching a candle melt in real time.

His steps dragged. His breaths were shallow. Every so often, I saw him blink like it took effort just to keep his eyes open.

CJ was watching him more than he was watching the road.

We both were.

He hadn't said a word since Shaun told him not to look like he was already gone.

But I could feel the war inside him.

Shaun tripped once — just once. His foot caught on the lip of a broken curb. He caught himself fast, waved us off. But I saw his face.

He wasn't okay.

He was barely here.

And CJ…

CJ couldn't take it.

He slowed his pace again, falling beside Shaun. Close, but not too close. He didn't want to spook him. Didn't want to make it worse.

"Still breathing?" CJ asked softly.

Shaun nodded once. "Barely."

CJ gave a tiny laugh. It wasn't happy. Just habit. Just history. "Sounds about right."

I kept ahead, giving them room. Giving them privacy in a world that no longer offered it.

And then I saw it.

Up ahead.

Across the intersection — a wide, open stretch of road leading toward the rise in the city where the extraction point waited.

It should've looked like hope.

It didn't.

Because at the far end of that road…

I saw movement.

Not infected.

Not a horde.

A pattern.

Deliberate. Controlled.

Stalking.

I froze.

CJ looked up. "What is it?"

I didn't answer right away.

Just stared through the grime-stained air.

"It's not over," I said finally.

Shaun coughed behind me. "It never is."

The street betrayed us.

We were halfway across the cracked open stretch when the silence broke — a howl from the rooftops, a biter leaping from behind a collapsed sedan.

Then came the wave.

No buildup.

No warning.

Just death from every angle.

Shaun barely had time to lift his blade before one hit him square in the chest. I got there first—one hand, no leverage—grabbed the thing by the collar with my elbow and slammed it into the car's hood. I drove my knife into its skull, teeth clenched so hard I thought I'd break them.

"Go!" I shouted. "Get him moving!"

CJ carved two down with a piece of pipe, yelling over the chaos. "This way—through the storefront!"

Shaun stumbled behind him, hand clutched over his ribs, blood already soaking through.

I stayed close.

Used my body as a shield.

I couldn't reload. I couldn't brace. But I could kill.

And I did — over and over.

They swarmed the sidewalk behind us.

We pulled into a destroyed storefront. Half a wall left, the floor a graveyard of glass and torn shelving. Shaun collapsed against a fallen beam, wheezing, pale.

CJ cleared the rear with a piece of concrete and a prayer. "That's it! That's all of them!"

But Shaun didn't get up.

He slid down the wall, breathing in rattled bursts, hand still pressed to the bite in his side.

CJ dropped beside him. "We're so close. Shaun—stay with me."

Shaun looked up, eyes dull but burning. "It's time."

CJ shook his head fast. "Don't say it."

"I'm not gonna make it."

CJ's breath hitched.

I stayed close, blade still slick in my one good hand.

We were too late.

And Shaun knew it.

CJ looked around — frantic, helpless — and spotted something in the debris.

A small, dust-covered tactical kit. Black. Cracked.

Inside — a grenade.

He pulled it out. Held it tight.

Didn't speak.

Just looked at Shaun.

Shaun saw it.

And nodded.

CJ held it forward.

Shaun reached for it with a shaking hand and took it.

Then pulled something from around his neck.

His dog tags.

He pressed them into CJ's hand. "You make it."

CJ's voice cracked. "You don't have to do this."

Shaun met his eyes. "There's no other way."

Then he pushed off the beam and stood.

Wobbling.

Bleeding.

But standing.

He limped into the street.

I moved to follow — instinct — but CJ held me back.

"He's choosing this," CJ said.

And I knew he was right.

Shaun faced the incoming infected — Ten of them, charging hard.

He didn't flinch.

He tore through the first one with a scream, elbowed the second, gutted the third, and bitten

by the fourth and fifth.

He screamed in pain.

Blood flew.

His knees buckled, but he stayed standing.

And then he turned.

Back toward us.

Back toward his brother.

And lifted the grenade.

Then he pulled the pin.

He held it up—just for a moment.

A soldier's salute.

And the blast hit.

But it wasn't clean.

It didn't kill him.

It blew off his arm.

Shaun collapsed.

The infected tore into him like he was nothing.

He screamed once.

And then he was gone.

CJ broke.

I held him back.

We watched Shaun die.

Because he chose to.

And we kept breathing—

Because he made damn sure we could.

18

SECTION ONE: CARRY IT ALL

He didn't speak at first.

Not when we pulled away from the ruins of Shaun's last stand.

Not when the wind picked up, and the sky turned the color of an open wound.

CJ just walked.

One hand on the pipe, still slick with blood.

The other curled around Shaun's dog tags, now clipped with his own.

They clinked with every step.

I wanted to say something — anything.

But I didn't.

Because whatever CJ was carrying… it was everything.

And I could feel it pressing down on both of us.

His shoulders were squared, his jaw locked, his steps exact. Every few feet, I heard him whisper under his breath. Just three words.

"Complete the mission."

Over and over.

Like a mantra.

Like a promise.

I kept up beside him, limping slightly, knife still in my one good hand. I'd offered to lead once — just once.

He looked at me like I'd insulted a ghost.

"I got you," he said.

That was it.

And I knew better than to question him again.

He scanned rooftops. Intersections. The skyline ahead. Every shadow, every sound — nothing got past him now.

He was no longer the sarcastic older child.

No longer the fixer.

CJ had become a sentinel.

And I… I just kept moving.

Trying not to think about the tags clinking beside him.

Trying not to picture Charles.

Or Sheila.

Or Shaun.

Trying not to be the last dead weight they gave their lives for.

"Complete the mission."

He said it again — this time louder.

Then glanced at me.

"You stay close. We're finishing this."

I nodded.

Because the fire behind his eyes wasn't just rage anymore.

It was a legacy.

The road narrowed into a crumbling overpass — one more ruin between us and the edge of this nightmare. Wind howled between the broken concrete beams like the city itself was exhaling.

We stopped in the shadow of a jackknifed military transport, long since looted, half its frame rusted into the ground. The silence there was deep. The kind that begs for something real to break it.

I reached into my jacket.

Pulled out two pieces of metal.

They'd never felt heavier.

I stepped toward CJ, slow.

He was kneeling beside a fire-scorched curb, checking his pipe weapon, muttering again.

"Complete the mission."

"CJ," I said.

He looked up.

His face was drawn, eyes hollow but locked in.

I opened my hand.

Two dog tags.

Scorched edges. Worn letters.

Sheila.

Charles.

His parents.

His war.

His burden.

He didn't say anything.

Just stared at them for a long moment.

I didn't speak either. There was nothing to say that wouldn't ruin it.

Finally, CJ reached out with trembling fingers.

Took them both.

He clipped them to his own chain — now four sets swaying together.

He didn't break down.

Didn't cry.

Didn't even blink.

He just stood. Taller somehow.

"Let's move," he said.

I nodded.

And as he stepped forward, I heard the tags clink once against his chest.

A sound I'll never forget.

The sound of what we carried now.

I stopped counting how many we faced.

Didn't matter anymore.

All I could do was keep my eyes on CJ.

Because he didn't stop.

We crossed the overpass into the teeth of another horde — silent at first, then shrieking, limbs flailing, jaws split wide with the hunger of the dead.

CJ walked straight into them.

And they didn't stand a chance.

His pipe cracked the skull of the first one so hard I felt it in my chest. He turned and buried it in the ribs of another, twisting as he pulled free. His blade came next — slicing across faces, through necks, painting the road in motion.

He didn't hesitate.

He didn't speak.

He just killed.

Deliberate.

Precise.

Furious.

One biter grabbed his shoulder — CJ snapped its arm with a twist, yanked it forward, and drove his knife up through its chin until the tip punched through the top of its skull.

Another came from behind — he spun, caught it by the throat, slammed it into a rusted barricade, and caved its head in with the pipe.

"CJ!" I yelled from behind him as a runner charged me.

I tried to get my knife up—too slow.

CJ was faster.

He turned, shoulder-checked the thing off course, and drove his blade through its spine.

Didn't even look at me when it fell.

"Keep up," he muttered.

That was it.

No speeches.

No pep talks.

Just blood and breath and purpose.

We crossed through the wreckage of a burned-out pharmacy. Three more came at once. CJ took all of them. One by one. Fast. Brutal.

The floor was slick. My one good hand was shaking. But I didn't fall.

Because he was ahead of me.

Clearing every path.

Fighting like Shaun was still beside him.

Like Charles was watching.

Like Sheila was still feeding him directions.

He wasn't running on adrenaline.

He was running on legacy.

I heard him whisper it again under his breath — teeth clenched.

"Complete the mission."

And I knew he wasn't stopping for anything.

Not until I was out.

Or he was dead.

The extraction tower finally appeared in the haze — battered, broken, but standing.

A signal flare sputtered above it like a dying heartbeat.

And between us and it?

A final wall of death.

Not just biters.

Smarter.

Faster.

Coordinated.

They stood between collapsed barricades, crouched on rusted military vehicles, their heads twitching, eyes locked. Waiting.

CJ saw them.

And didn't stop.

He reached for his chest, fingers brushing the four sets of dog tags now clinking together with every step.

Sheila. Charles. Shaun. And his own.

He grabbed the chain like a lifeline.

Then looked back at me.

"This is it."

I nodded. My hand trembled on my knife hilt — my only hand, my only weapon.

"I've got your back," I said.

CJ didn't smile.

He just said, "I know."

Then he ran.

Straight into the final swarm.

They reacted fast — too fast — teeth bared, arms lashing out.

CJ ducked under the first, jammed his pipe into its throat, and spun, slamming his shoulder into a second. His blade came out in a blur, slashing across one face, stabbing another in the eye.

I moved behind him, striking low, sweeping legs, jamming metal into torsos where I could. I wasn't clean. I wasn't fast.

But I wasn't dead.

Because CJ kept clearing the way.

Two more grabbed at him from behind — he ripped one off by the jaw and hurled it into the side of a transport truck. The other bit at his shoulder — he rolled, twisted, stabbed three times until it went limp.

He was bleeding.

Breath ragged.

But his feet didn't stop.

"Keep going!" he shouted.

I stumbled behind him, swung upward with my blade and dropped another charging infected.

The signal tower was close now — the tarmac visible through smoke and wreckage.

I turned just in time to see CJ shove a flaming corpse off the road and vault over a fallen barrier.

We hit the last intersection—

And the horde collapsed on us from both sides.

CJ turned and shielded me with his body.

He gritted his teeth and roared through the fire and blood, slicing, slamming, swinging—

Until there was no one left standing but us.

The last two infected clawed toward him.

CJ ran straight through them.

Pipe. Blade. Elbow.

They didn't get back up.

I couldn't breathe. I couldn't feel my legs. But I saw it.

The clearing ahead.

Extraction.

CJ turned, chest heaving, eyes burning.

The dog tags around his neck clinked together.

I'll never forget the sound.

Then he pointed forward.

His voice cracked. Raw. Final.

"Run."

There it was.

The extraction point.

A battered landing pad just ahead, wrapped in smoke and lit by the flicker of a weak signal flare.

And above it — like a vision we didn't trust yet — the chopper.

Spinning blades.

Dust kicked up around it.

Still waiting.

Still there.

CJ stopped first.

His chest was heaving. His blade arm hung low. The pipe in his other hand trembled. But when he saw the helicopter, something inside him almost gave out.

We had made it.

After everything — after Sheila, after Charles, after Shaun — we were finally here.

CJ looked over at me.

Didn't speak.

Just nodded.

And then—

We felt it.

That shift in the air.

The stillness that wasn't peace.

That wasn't relief.

I turned.

So did CJ.

And there it stood.

At the edge of the wreckage, rising from the fog like it had been waiting for this exact moment—

It.

The one we hadn't seen clearly.

The one that had been behind the scout's scream, the collapsing towers, the shifting hordes.

The intelligence beneath the chaos.

It was tall.

Wrong.

Twisted in ways that didn't make sense — like it had once been human, but had evolved past the rules of skin and bone.

Its limbs were lean, stretched. Its ribs flared out like armor.

Its mouth was sealed shut with jagged bone.

But its eyes—

God, its eyes were alive.

Watching.

Calculating.

CJ muttered, "What the fuck…"

It didn't charge.

Didn't snarl.

It just took a step forward.

And another.

Slow. Measured.

CJ raised his blade.

I raised mine.

The helicopter was still behind us.

But this thing?

It was here for us.

Not like the others.

Not for hunger.

For the end.

THE LAST MILE OF DIABLO FOUR

It didn't move like the others.

It didn't rush. It didn't roar.

It just watched.

Its head tilted, bones shifting beneath stretched grey skin.

Every step it took echoed like it was counting down to something.

CJ stood in front of me, body squared, pipe in one hand, blade in the other. He didn't breathe hard anymore. Didn't blink.

He just stared back.

"No jokes," I muttered.

CJ didn't turn. "No time."

I could hear the helicopter's engine whining louder in the distance, blades cutting the air, screaming for us to run.

But this thing — this twisted monster — was all that stood between us and the sky.

It took another step forward.

CJ reached for his radio. "Eagle One, this is Diablo Four. Begin lift prep. The package is approaching LZ."

Copy that, Diablo Four. Wheels hot. Two minutes max.

CJ lowered the mic. "Run, Mr. President."

I didn't move.

His voice hardened. "That wasn't a suggestion."

"I'm not leaving you."

CJ turned to me for the first time. His eyes — hollow, burned, ready — didn't ask for understanding.

Only trust.

"Shaun died to get you here. My mom. My dad. I'm not letting it be for nothing."

Behind us, the chopper blades kicked into full rotation.

Dust and ash swirled in the air.

He looked back at the creature, now inches closer.

Its mouth began to open, bones cracking.

Not to scream.

To breathe us in.

CJ stepped forward. "I'll hold it."

"CJ—"

He grabbed my vest with one hand and shoved me back toward the rising landing pad.

"GO!"

I turned and ran.

And behind me, I heard him charge.

No more fear.

No more words.

Just the final mile of Diablo Four.

The ramp was already lowering when I reached the helicopter.

Wind slashed against my face. Dust and blood smeared across my vision.

I stumbled, tripped — the crew inside grabbed my vest and hauled me up with a yell.

"Clear! Clear! Get us in the air!"

But I turned.

Back toward the hell behind me.

CJ.

He was still fighting.

Still holding that thing back.

His pipe was gone.

Just his blade now — and blood.

Too much blood.

The mutant lunged. CJ dodged left, slashed across its chest, but it didn't stop. It moved like a shadow through fire. Twisting. Silent.

"CJ!" I screamed.

He didn't look.

He ran.

Full sprint toward the helicopter.

The thing chased him.

The ramp started to lift.

CJ jumped.

His hand caught the edge. Slipped.

He fell—

I caught him.

One hand.

Every nerve in my arm screamed. The pressure tore through my shoulder like it would rip me in half. His body swung, feet dangling, eyes wild.

"Pull me up!" he shouted.

I gritted my teeth and pulled.

And that's when it happened.

The creature launched.

It caught CJ's leg midair—

 And bit down.

CJ's scream tore through the rotor wash.

The pilot shouted over the comms. "WE CAN'T LIFT — TOO MUCH WEIGHT!"

We started tilting. Dropping.

CJ looked up at me — pain carved deep into every line of his face.

And then, slowly…

He smiled.

The helicopter dipped hard.

Wind howled.

The pilot shouted, "We're too heavy! He's gotta let go!"

But CJ was still hanging from the edge.

One hand gripped mine.

His leg — bitten, torn open. Blood dripping like rain.

I held him with my one good hand, arm shaking, shoulder screaming, feet braced against the ramp floor.

His eyes met mine.

And instead of fear…

He smiled.

Not peace.

Closure.

He reached down with his free hand, fumbled at his chest — four tags, clinking on the chain: Sheila. Charles. Shaun. Himself.

He pulled the chain free.

But he didn't hand them to me.

He bent forward, shaking, eyes clenched with pain, and tucked them into my boot — sliding them in just deep enough that I'd never lose them.

Then he looked up again.

"Cj, don't do this," I whispered.

CJ smiled wider. Bloody teeth. Tears in his eyes.

Then he took a breath—

And said it:

"This is Echo Black… signing out."

"Mission accomplished."

Then he let go.

I lunged — but I couldn't catch him.

He dropped like steel through smoke, hit the concrete below with a sickening thud—

And then stood.

Bleeding. Broken. But not done.

The mutant stepped toward him.

CJ limped forward, blade gripped tight.

One last scream tore from his chest as he charged it.

He drove the knife into its side, snarling. It slammed him back.

Three more infected hit him at once.

CJ roared, fighting back like a man already dead, teeth bared, blood flying.

He took one with him.

Then another.

Then the mutant's claws came down—

And Echo Black was gone.

20

THE FAMILY I ONCE KNEW

They said the infected were gone.

For the first time in months, the city skyline didn't scream. No smoke in the air. No gunfire in the distance. Just scaffolding, hammering, and the slow grind of hope coming back to life.

I stood backstage, surrounded by silence.

The podium waited in front of me. Cameras are already rolling. The crowd buzzing in anticipation just beyond the curtain — survivors, soldiers, press. The ones who made it.

And behind me—

Small fingers laced into my remaining hand.

I looked down.

Emma.

My daughter.

She wore a pale blue jacket too big for her, sleeves rolled up, golden hair pulled back behind her ears. Ten years old. Brave in a way I'll never understand.

She smiled up at me.

And I couldn't stop my knees from going weak.

I dropped to one knee — my only hand cradling her cheek.

She looked older now.

The world had taken months from her, I could never give back.

"I missed you, Daddy."

My voice barely worked. "I missed you more."

She hugged me.

Tight. Fierce. Like she knew what I'd been through without needing the words.

And tucked inside my chest—

Four dog tags clinked against one another.

A family I'll never see again.

The curtain parted.

The noise hit me like a wave — applause, camera flashes, movement from the edges of the crowd. Survivors. Doctors. Military. Children on shoulders. People are finally daring to believe in tomorrow.

They didn't cheer like I was a leader.

They cheered like I was proof that humanity still existed.

I stepped up to the podium.

One hand gripped the edge to steady myself — the stump of the other wrapped in a clean cuff beneath my suit.

Emma stood behind me, just out of frame, watched by two Secret Service agents who didn't look nearly as tough as her.

I scanned the sea of faces.

And the weight hit all over again.

Four sets of dog tags pressed against my chest, tucked inside the lining of my coat.

I'd carried them every day since.

Even when it hurt to breathe. Even when nightmares clawed at my ribs. Even when I woke up screaming.

I took a breath.

The cameras focused.

The crowd hushed.

My mouth opened.

And then closed.

I looked down.

Then up.

And I smiled.

Not for the world.

For them.

I looked at them all.

Hundreds of faces.

Thousands more are watching from screens across the world.

Waiting for answers.

Waiting for hope.

Waiting for something that sounded like an ending.

I felt the weight of the tags over my heart.

One hand tucked into my coat.

My daughter standing behind me — alive because of them.

I leaned forward.

Took the mic.

And then said—

"Before I begin…"

A pause.

One deep breath.

"…I know what you're all expecting. I know you want to hear about the cure. About how it works. How we're rebuilding. How the nightmare finally ended."

My voice cracked — not from nerves from memory.

"But before I get into all that…"

I looked at the sea of eyes.

And thought of a grey-haired woman with a map always in her hand.

Of a man built like stone, whose voice could shake the dead.

Of two brothers — one who smiled through every hell we walked, and one who held the line until there was no line left.

"Let me tell you about the family I once knew."